P9-DIE-767

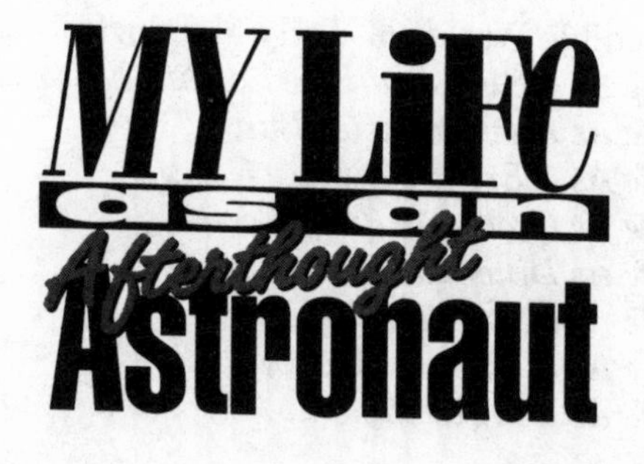
MY LiFE
as an
Afterthought
Astronaut

BOOKS BY BILL MYERS

Children's Series

McGee and Me! (12 books)

The Incredible Worlds of Wally McDoogle:
—*My Life As a Smashed Burrito with Extra Hot Sauce*
—*My Life As Alien Monster Bait*
—*My Life As a Broken Bungee Cord*
—*My Life As Crocodile Junk Food*
—*My Life As Dinosaur Dental Floss*
—*My Life As a Torpedo Test Target*
—*My Life As a Human Hockey Puck*
—*My Life As an Afterthought Astronaut*

Fantasy Series

Journeys to Fayrah:
—*The Portal*
—*The Experiment*
—*The Whirlwind*
—*The Tablet*

Teen Series

Forbidden Doors:
—*The Society*
—*The Deceived*
—*The Spell*
—*The Haunting*
—*The Guardian*
—*The Encounter*

Teen Books

Hot Topics, Tough Questions
Christ B.C.

the incredible worlds of Wally McDoogle

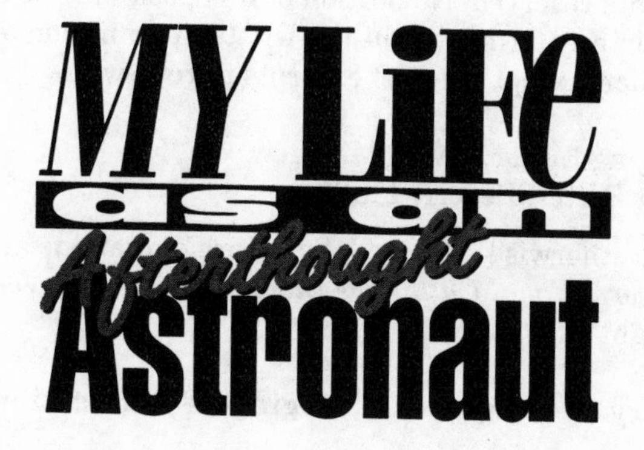

BILL MYERS

WORD PUBLISHING
Dallas • London • Vancouver • Melbourne

MY LIFE AS AN AFTERTHOUGHT ASTRONAUT

Copyright © 1995 by Bill Myers.

All rights reserved. No portion of this book may be reproduced in any form without the written permission of the publisher, except for brief excerpts in reviews.

Managing Editor: Laura Minchew
Project Editor: Beverly Phillips

Unless otherwise indicated, Scripture quotations are from the *International Children's Bible, New Century Version*, copyright © 1983, 1986, 1988.

Library of Congress Cataloging-in-Publication Data

Myers, Bill, 1953–
My life as an afterthought astronaut / Bill Myers.
p. cm. — (The incredible worlds of Wally McDoogle ; bk. 8)

Summary: When accident-prone Wally McDoogle finds himself a part of a space shuttle mission, he learns a lesson about the importance of obeying the rules.
ISBN 0–8499–3602–0
[1. Space shuttles—Fiction. 2. Christian life—Fiction. 3. Humorous stories.] I. Title. II. Series: Myers, Bill, 1953– Incredible worlds of Wally McDoogle ; #8.
PZ7.M98234Myt 1995
[Fic]—dc20 94–45373
CIP
AC

Printed in the United States of America

97 98 99 00 QBP 9 8

To Bill Greig III, Linda Holland, Christy Weir, Kyle Duncan, and Mark Maddox, who encouraged me to "launch" this series.

"Whoever obeys the commands protects his life.
Whoever is careless in what he does will die."

—Proverbs 19:16

Contents

Chapter 1

Just for Starters . . .

Just 'cause I didn't follow the rules doesn't make it my fault that the Space Shuttle almost crashed.

Well, okay, maybe that was sort of my fault.

But not the part when Pilot O'Brien was spacewalking and I accidentally knocked him halfway to Jupiter, or when I wound up in a space suit and nearly became the first human satellite to orbit the Earth; you can't blame that on me.

Well, okay, maybe that was sort of my fault, too.

But it wasn't my fault that Wall Street sold me a root beer. And when you get right down to it, that was really how the whole mess began. . . .

We were touring the Kennedy Space Center in Florida. It was one of those family vacation things Dad always dreams up. Last year he dragged us to a bunch of old battlefields where a bunch of old battles took place. Wonderful. Almost as exciting as watching grass grow. The year before that, we took the Great Caves of America tour. Not bad, if you happened to have brought along plenty of comic books and a flashlight to read them by.

This year my older brothers, Burt and Brock, dreamed up some great excuses not to go. Burt said he wanted to attend Hula Dancing School—(he thought being the only guy student in a class with three hundred beautiful babes might be kind of interesting. Go figure.) And Brock, never the smarter of the two, decided on Dental Floss Camp—(something about all those free dental floss samples he'd been getting. I told you he wasn't so bright.)

At any rate, that left two openings—one for my best friend Wall Street, who wants to make her first million by age fourteen, and the other one for my other best friend Opera, the human eating machine.

We had done the usual Florida touristy things. We went to Epcot Center and sweated . . . Disney World and sweated . . . the beach and sweated, Universal Studios and sweated, and so on. Same crowds, same sweat. And then, just when we figured we'd sweated all the sweat we could ever sweat, Dad remembered The Kennedy Space Sauna . . . er, I mean, Center.

We were bushed. There is something about three best friends vacationing together that means getting to bed around 4:30 A.M. each day and waking up about 4:33 A.M. Not a bad deal if you don't mind sleepwalking through the day.

In between catnaps, I remember the Space Center being pretty cool. In fact, they were getting ready to launch the new space shuttle, the *Encounter*, so there were lots of people running around looking important. But nobody was looking more important than our tour guide, Ms. Durkelbuster.

"Don't touch this, don't touch that, stay in line, lower your voices, don't speak to anyone unless they speak to you." The poor lady obviously wanted to be in charge of something, and since there were no openings for Supreme World Dictator, I guess she had to settle for being our tour guide.

"Standing before you is the Launch Control Center," she shouted through a blow horn.

We looked up at the giant four-story building that towered above us. Luckily there was a strong breeze, so we weren't excreting our normal quota of sweat. Lucky for us, unlucky for Ms. Durkelbuster. I guess when you use half a can of hair spray to plaster down every hair, you don't appreciate Mother Nature's little experiments with hair styling. As a neat freak, the poor woman was constantly readjusting her hair, while all the time making sure we stood perfectly silent, in a perfect semicircle, while she recited her perfectly memorized speech: "There are four separate firing rooms within this structure. At this moment ninety-four skilled scientists are in these rooms observing every detail of the countdown."

Another gust of wind hit and messed up another one of her ultra-varnished hairs. She quickly pulled it down and bent it back into place. "Before we enter the firing rooms, it is imperative that you leave all food and beverages outside. There are hundreds of computers as well as sensitive electrical equipment within those walls. One misplaced crumb or spilled beverage could jeopardize the entire mission."

As we entered the building (in perfect single file, of course), everyone obeyed the rules and dumped their stuff in the outside trash. Everyone but me. I was dying of thirst. And since I'd bought a root beer from Wall Street at a price just under the cost of the entire space program (I told you she knew how to make a buck), I figured smuggling the can inside for a drink couldn't hurt.

That was my first mistake. My second mistake

was trying to hide the can. As we headed up the stairs, I stuffed it into my shorts pocket. A good idea, except this particular pair of shorts didn't have pockets (a detail I might have remembered if I hadn't been sleepwalking). The can fell to the ground and bounced halfway down the flight of steps.

K-LINK, K-LANK, K-RUNK, K-LUNK!

Fortunately, Ms. Durkelbuster was too busy rearranging her plasticized bangs to notice. I ran down the steps and grabbed the can. It was a little dented from all the excitement, but it was still in pretty good shape . . . at least on the outside. I had no idea what all that bouncing had done on the inside.

Ms. Durkelbuster opened the door, and we stepped into a room just slightly bigger than Cleveland. The place had more monitors than a video arcade. Everyone was wearing headsets and looking very official. But not as official as Ms. Durkelbuster, who seemed to swell with every word: "Welcome one and all to NASA's Launch Control."

At the front of the room was a huge glass window. Through it you could see the *Encounter*, which was waiting for tomorrow morning's liftoff. As everyone oohed and ahhed and took pictures, I thought I'd take a drink.

While Ms. Durkelbuster continued rambling on about tomorrow's mission and the tons of electronic junk that would do the tons of electronic stuff, I carefully reached for the can's aluminum tab. I lifted it as gently as a bomb expert defusing a bomb.

Unfortunately, this bomb went off.

All that stair bouncing had definitely taken its toll. When I popped the top, foam shot through the opening. And we're not talking a little fizz, here. We're talking a major, look out!-it's-Old-Faithful, root-beer geyser!

People screamed and leaped aside. So did I. Unfortunately, I leaped aside right into a fire alarm box on the wall. No problem, except the part where I accidentally broke the little glass rod, which accidentally set off the alarm, which sent even more people scurrying.

But not Ms. Durkelbuster. Having been trained for every emergency, she grabbed a fire extinguisher and shouted, "Step aside! I'm a professional! I will handle this!"

"There's nothing to handle!" I yelled over the alarm. "It's just this can of—"

But Ms. Durkelbuster had no time for facts. She was too busy trying to be a hero. A fire alarm was sounding, and her training clearly stated that fire alarms called for fire extinguishers. She pointed the nozzle at me and—

"You don't understand," I shouted, "It's just my root—"

WHOOSH . . .

I was suddenly covered in three feet of foam.

That was the good news. The bad news was when the powerful stream of foam hit my can, it knocked it out of my hand, smashing my little gusher bomb against the wall, where it ricocheted right back at her, spraying the sticky brew all over her.

"AUGH!" she screamed. "My hair, my hair!"

But we weren't done yet. Oh, no. After all, we are talking about Wally If-It-Can-Go-Wrong-Count-On-It-Going-Wrong McDoogle. Like a bad, slow-motion dream, the can sailed over her head toward a nearby computer console (spewing its satisfying refreshment in all directions). It finally crashed into the terminal and poured out the rest of its contents.

It was quite a sight. There were more sparks than on the Fourth of July. And, as the security guards grabbed me and the dripping Ms. Durkelbuster, I began to suspect it was not going to be one of my better days.

* * * * *

Forty-five minutes later I was sitting by myself outside the Launch Control Center. Ms.

Durkelbuster was busy cleaning out her locker and buying a newspaper, so she could go through the Help-Wanted section. Before we parted, I suggested she look into becoming a hair stylist. She suggested I stay out of her way before she broke my face.

Dad was almost as mad. He made it clear that just because *I* broke the rules was no reason for the rest of the family to suffer. I could sit outside the building and think about my behavior until the tour was over.

That was fine with me. It would give me a chance to catch a few Z's, tune up my tan, and, of course, sweat. I had thought of starting a new superhero story on ol' Betsy, the laptop computer that I always carry around, but I was just too tired.

I closed my eyes and was just dropping into a nice state of unconsciousness when I heard them: another tour group coming out of the building. I opened my eyes. They were about the size of my group, but instead of the little tags that had "Visitor" printed on them, these guys all had cool badges that had "V.I.P." (Very Important People) printed on them. The badges were cool, but not as cool as what their tour guide was saying: "Now you must understand what we're about to do is very unusual. Going up and visiting the shuttle this close to launch is *never* permitted."

My ears perked up. Had I heard right? Were these people actually going to visit the shuttle? I leaned forward to listen as they filed past me toward a special bus with the same V.I.P. letters plastered on the front.

The guide continued, "But since you're all friends and relatives of the Senator, and since he is such a great supporter of the space program, we have permission to take a quick peek and break the rules just this once."

I had my answer. Without thinking (one of my better skills), I leaped from the bench, grabbed ol' Betsy, and joined the end of the line. No way would they notice one more kid. No way was I going to miss seeing the shuttle. And if they were going to "break the rules just this once," no way could they not count me in.

Unfortunately, I'd soon wish they had counted me out.

Chapter 2

A Little Sleepover

As the bus headed for the launch site, the new tour guide, who was about 3002% nicer than Ms. Durkelbuster, rattled off a few hundred dos and don'ts. Little things, like not lighting up a cigarette around the seven gazillion gallons of rocket fuel unless you enjoyed being vaporized in a gazillionth of a second. Or, when we arrived at the shuttle, not to reach inside and press any buttons, especially those labeled: "Launch."

She also joked about the tour having twenty-seven people in it and that she expected to count twenty-seven heads when we were all done, just in case anyone had sudden cravings to become a stowaway.

Of course, everyone chuckled. So did I. Not over the joke, but over the knowledge that the group no longer had twenty-seven people, but twenty-eight.

We climbed out of the bus and squeezed into an elevator that rose slower than Mom drives when there's a police car behind her. There wasn't much to see. Just the usual cables, metal framework, pipes, and billion-dollar rocket engines.

"The two smaller rockets on each side have solid fuel in them," our guide explained. "During liftoff they are the first to be jettisoned and will parachute 150 miles off of the coast where a ship will recover them and bring them back for reuse. The large orange tank you see in the middle is mostly liquid oxygen and hydrogen. It will be jettisoned a little later and will burn up in the atmosphere."

Suddenly a hand shot up so fast that I thought someone had to go to the bathroom. In reality it was just one of those showoffs (I guess every group has to have one) who was trying to impress us all with his staggering knowledge. "Actually," he said, "the precise time of External Tank Separation is at 8 minutes and 54 seconds into the flight, is it not?"

Our tour leader forced a smile. "Yes, that's correct."

Showoff looked around, beaming at us. No one bothered to beam back.

Finally, the elevator jolted to a stop. Before us was a narrow steel bridge that led to the shuttle. Everyone stared in hushed awe.

"Okay," our guide said, "before we head down that ramp there are a couple more things you should know. First, you must not touch the spacecraft. In fact, it's prohibited for anyone to come within three feet of the vehicle."

Before anybody could complain or Showoff could convert the three feet into metric units, the guide continued. "However, I have asked one of the technicians to open the hatch for us, so you'll at least be able to see the mid deck where the crew will carry out many of their experiments. You'll also be able to see the ladder that leads up to the flight deck where the pilot and commander fly the shuttle."

Everybody was impressed. Everybody except Showoff. "There are actually three levels to the crew's compartment. You mentioned only two."

"Well, yes," our guide answered, having a harder time finding her smile. "Technically, there are three. There is also a lower deck that can be reached by removing some floor panels of the mid deck. It's basically a storage area and the location of the life support systems."

Mr. Know-It-All grinned as if he'd be able to sleep better knowing the oversight had been cleared up.

Our guide continued. "I will have to ask you to please remove everything from your shirt pockets—pencils, papers, anything that could fall out."

I glanced into my pocket and saw nothing but

the remains of the last dinner my little sister cooked—cremated cauliflower. It's a known fact that if you don't want to hurt someone's feelings, shirt pockets are a great place to hide their attempts at cooking. I quickly dumped the rock-hard pebbles out of my pocket.

But our guide wasn't through yet. "Also any rings, watches, or eyeglasses should be removed."

Uh-oh. Without my glasses I couldn't see the broad side of a barn door. Come to think of it, I couldn't see the barn, either. But if I raised my hand and protested, I'd draw attention to myself—a definite no-no if you're trying to blend into the crowd.

So, reluctantly, I took off the ol' specs. But I kept them carefully hidden in my hand. I knew if I waited and hung back at the end of the line, there was always a chance no one would notice me slipping them on to take a peek. Of course, that would mean breaking another rule, but so far this rule-breaking business had been paying off pretty well.

We headed down the long steel ramp as everyone whispered in excitement. I pulled up the rear, doing my best Helen Keller imitation, while assuring the girl in front of me, the one whose back I kept groping, that I was not trying to be fresh.

Next, we arrived in a small white room. Just a few feet away stood the shuttle entrance. Each person approached and looked through the hatch before turning and heading back. At last it was my turn. The plan worked perfectly. Everybody else had turned and was heading back, so I quickly slipped on my glasses to take a look.

Well, at least that's what I tried to do. But, as you may remember, I'm not the world's most coordinated person. Some people find it hard to walk and chew gum at the same time. Not me. I've never been able to get the gum out of the wrapper.

As I reached up to put on my glasses, they slipped from my hands. No problem, till I tried to catch them. Even that wasn't a problem, except for the part where I accidentally knocked them through the hatch's opening and into the shuttle.

"*Oops.*"

It was decision time. Should I break another rule and step inside to get them? As I said, this rule-breaking business was going pretty well, so I figured, sure, why not?

I quickly stepped through the opening and into the shuttle. The place looked fantastic. It looked even more fantastic when I found my glasses, slipped them on, and could actually see it. Everything was all white with lots of little compartment doors and switches and stuff. And, directly in front of me was the ladder which our guide had explained led to the flight deck.

I turned to the group. Everyone was heading back down the ramp toward the elevator. (The fact that Mr. Know-It-All was now giving a lecture on the composition of the shuttle's hull probably helped hurry them on.) In any case, no one looked back.

I turned to the ladder. It would only take a second to climb. Just a second to check out the flight deck with all those cool controls and stuff.

And since I was already on board . . .

It was definitely risky and definitely against the rules. So, of course, I definitely did it. I scampered up the ladder and took a quick peek.

Wow! It was like the cockpit of one of those big jetliners. There were two seats up front, the commander's and the pilot's. They were surrounded by billions of buttons and controls. There were also plenty of computer screens.

I don't know how long I stood there staring. But I knew I couldn't push my luck any further, so I turned and started back down the ladder. At least that's what I wanted to do. Unfortunately, ol' Betsy had other ideas. Somehow, with all my crawling around, I got her shoulder strap hung up on a little black handle beside the commander's seat.

I tried to unhook it, but I only made matters worse. Soon I had created a giant knot. And since my knot-untying abilities rate right up there with the rest of my coordination skills, a slight problem was developing. In no time flat, I had tied the shoulder strap into a beautiful pretzel-like design. Nice, if you wanted to hang a plant by it or give it to Aunt Martha for Christmas—lousy if you wanted to get out of a space shuttle with it.

And then it happened. . . .

There I was, trying to untie the strap (which was looking more and more like a nicely crocheted sweater) when, suddenly, I heard the hatch down on the mid deck slam.

I finally managed to slip the tangled strap off the handle. Then I crawled down the ladder as fast as I could, but I was too late. The door was sealed shut.

Uh-oh . . .

I thought about banging on the hatch and screaming for my life. I also thought about spending the next hundred years of that life in some federal prison and finally getting out only to have Dad ground me for another hundred years. Call me crazy, but I figured there had to be another way.

But what?

* * * * *

An hour later, after checking out the inside of the shuttle a few million times, I boldly climbed back into the commander's chair. I, the great Wally McDoogle, had a plan. . . .

All I had to do was sit tight and wait for the sound of a technician reopening the hatch down on the mid deck. When I heard that, I'd jump up, wait until the guy turned his back, then climb down the ladder and run for all I was worth. (Which, if I were caught, would be about 32 cents.)

In the meantime, all I had to do was wait. To help keep my mind off the problem and to try to relax a little, I thought I'd write another one of my superhero stories. Forget the shrinks, the tranquilizers, the group therapy sessions. Whenever I'm feeling a little tense, nothing beats a good escape into the imaginary world I create on my laptop computer.

I pulled ol' Betsy out of her case, snapped her on, and started typing. . . .

It is just another average evening in Boringville, where...

—Average kids are tucked into average beds and being read average bedtime stories.

—Average moms are loading average dishwashers with plates crusted in average food.

—Average teenagers are complaining about emptying their average cats' average cat boxes.

Sadly, our hero, the above-average (and always stylishly dressed) Neutron Dude enters the deserted nuclear reactor he now calls home. It is a lonely life for our superhero. Being more radioactive than a hydrogen bomb has its drawbacks—especially in an average town like Boringville.

Oh sure, he was everybody's friend this afternoon, back when they needed him to fire a sneeze of his neutron breath at the fleet of flying cows invading from the planet Moojuice. (They didn't mind the cows; it was the cowpies that made them a little nervous.)

And, of course, they loved him when the school's microwave went on the fritz and he zapped their 234 hamburger casseroles so everyone could have a hot lunch.

And let's not forget all those glow-in-the dark wall sticker stars that keep getting recharged every time he passes by Boringville homes.

But try letting our hero live an average life with these average people of

Boringville and you could just forget it....

First, he tried buying a house in the little community. The neighbors complained that his glow kept them awake at night.

Next, he moved to a farm. The country folks complained their remote TVs changed channels every time he hiccuped.

Finally, there was that unfortunate incident with the neighbor's dog. It wasn't Neutron Guy's fault that ol' Muttley bit into his leg and got the "shock of his life." Talk about a "hot dog." You could see the smoke for miles.

Let's face it, our poor superhero just wasn't average enough to fit in.

Neutron Dude heads to the kitchen to drown his sorrows in some heaping helpings of horrendously unhealthy (and oh, so tasty) junkfood. Yes sir, nothing numbs the pain like pure unadulterated, empty carbos. He walks to the first cupboard and opens it. There, in all of their wonderful, tooth-decaying goodness, is his stash of Chewy-Gooey bars.

But, just as he reaches for a bar, there

is a blinding flash of light followed by some pretty cool sci-fi sound effects.

Our good guy looks around. Everything seems normal. But what about that flash and those cool sound effects? With a superhero shrug, he returns to his snack only to discover (*Da-da-DAAAA*—that, of course is cool sci-fi music) he is no longer reaching for a Chewy-Gooey. He is grabbing a very large cucumber.

He steps back in confusion. He opens the next cupboard where he keeps his year's supply of Super Goobers. To his amazement they've also been changed. Now they're organically grown, so-healthy-you-could-throw-up, carrot sticks.

Neutron Dude swallows back a wave of revulsion. Such healthy goodness is more than he can stomach. He throws a look over to the candy dish on the table. To his horror, the cinnamon sticks have turned to celery sticks, and the M&Ms have become raisins!

Before things get any weirder (or the food any healthier) Neutron Dude's phone rings. He picks it up and answers, "Hello!"

"Greetings, Glow Boy."

Neutron Dude lights up in surprise as we hear another blast of music. (This time it's the bad guy theme). "Veggie-Man," our hero shouts. "Is this you?"

"Who else?"

"All of these fruits and vegetables, are they your doing?"

"Ditto, Fission Face."

"But, you're supposed to be in prison."

"I got out on parole because of my good eating habits."

"Don't tell me they fell for that old scam."

"That's right, Nuclear Nerd. They let me out early for cleaning my plate and—"

Neutron Dude knows what is coming, and he finishes the phrase "...for always eating your vegetables."

"Precisely," the voice chuckles.

Neutron Dude shudders a shivering shudder, then shivers a shuddering shiver. He had dealt with Veggie-Man years earlier when the madman tried to force the local potato chip factory into manufacturing broccoli chips. No one knows what made the crazy Veggie-Man such a health-food health nut. Some say it was his mom making him eat one too many Brussels sprouts for dinner. Others say it was those dancing vegetable puppets on TV kids shows. Then there's the theory of one too many diet informercials on TV. Whatever the reason, Veggie-Man's sole mission in life was to make sure no one ate anything but organically grown fruits and vegetables.

"I have returned to my laboratory," the mad scientist cackled. "And I have released a special spray into the atmosphere. Soon it will change all the world's food into health food."

"You don't mean—"

"That's right. Hamburgers will soon become Broccoliburgers."

"That's terrible."

"Milkshakes will become Cream of Spinach Shakes."

"You're making me sick!"

"And for Thanksgiving, plan on carving up a nice, hickory-smoked...cabbage (with lovely Lima bean dressing).

Before Neutron Dude has a chance to lose his cookies (or have them changed into rutabagas), Veggie-Man hangs up.

Not wanting to see this year's trick-or-treat bag filled with candied asparagus, our hero suddenly uses all his good-guy strength to transform himself into pure, don't-try-this-at-home-kids protons. He lifts up the receiver and prepares to leap into the phone, to zap through the lines and begin a city-wide search for the hideous health nut's laboratory.

Who knows what evil awaits? Who knows what low-cholesterol, fat-free weapons will be unleashed? Who knows how Wally will get out of this space shuttle?

I stopped and looked at the last line. I'd never had reality invade my superhero stories before. Not like this. I shook my head and pressed the delete key. I guess I was more worried about being stuck here than I thought. Or maybe I was just tired. Or maybe both. I gave a hearty yawn, punched F10 to save, and put ol' Betsy away.

It was time for some serious thinking. Unfortunately, all I could do was some serious yawning. I guess all those nights of staying up late with Opera and Wall Street were finally catching up. But I couldn't take the chance of dozing off here in the commander's chair. What if somebody came in and saw me?

I had to find someplace safe, someplace where I wouldn't be seen if I should nod off. But someplace where I could still make a run for it when they opened the hatch.

I started to search both decks of the shuttle. My eyes grew heavier by the second. Then, for some reason, I remembered what Mr. Know-It-All had said, something about there not being two decks on the shuttle, but three. Wasn't the third level supposed to be under some sort of floor panel on the mid deck?

In exactly 1.33 minutes I found the loose floor panel and pulled it up. There were lots of tanks and hoses and stuff, but I managed to squeeze in along with ol' Betsy. I gave another yawn, then pulled the panel back in place just a few inches above my face. Perfect. Not exactly the Holiday Inn, but at least I'd be safe. No one would stumble upon me.

I gave another yawn. I wasn't planning on going to sleep. I just wanted to give my eyes a quick rest. Come to think of it, though, forty winks wouldn't be such a bad idea. Actually, eighty might even be better. Then again, since I was so nice and cozy . . .

ZZZZZzzzzzzz . . .

Chapter 3

Up, Up, and Away . . .

It was another one of my strange dreams. Wally McDoogle's wacky imagination at its weirdest.

I dreamed I was either a giant fly pinned under a giant fly swatter . . . or a giant waffle being cooked in a giant waffle iron. (It's hard to get every detail straight with these kinds of dreams.) In any case, it wasn't a bad dream, except for the part where I couldn't move or breathe, and I felt totally trapped.

Suddenly the waffle iron (or fly swatter) began to vibrate. Then it tilted forward. Next, I was kicked in the back. But we're not talking about some little kid-sister kick. We're not even talking some mule or Mr.-Ed-the-Talking-Horse kick. We're talking a major, the-earth-leaned-back-and-hit-me-with-everything-it-had kind of kick. In fact it was so violent that it knocked me clean out of that dream and into another, even weirder one.

Now I dreamed I was taking off in the space shuttle. (I told you I had a weird imagination.) The rumble turned into a deafening roar followed by lots and lots of shaking. Soon, I was doing my famous, Wally the Human Pinball imitation as I rolled and bounced in every possible direction. Fortunately, the floor panel from the mid deck that I'd put back over me stopped some of the bouncing.

Floor panel!

Mid deck!

This wasn't one of my weird dreams. . . . IT WAS ONE OF MY WEIRDER REALITIES!

The noise grew worse. So did the shaking. And the louder and harder things shook, the more I was shoved backwards. We were moving! Taking off! The acceleration pushed down on my body, pulled back on my cheeks, and made my eyes water. It was worse than riding with my brother Brock when he's late for school. Suddenly I weighed a couple hundred pounds more than normal. I wanted to shout, but I knew nobody could hear me. I wasn't even sure I could hear me.

I don't know how long this lasted. All I know is that I said a couple of prayers, actually, a lot of prayers. Actually, I asked God to forgive me for everything I ever did from the moment I was born ("Sorry about wetting on that doctor when he spanked me"), up until I sneaked on board the shuttle, especially the sneaking on board the shuttle part. Let's face it, if you die, the last thing you want is to go to heaven with something like that on your permanent record.

Suddenly, all the noise and vibration stopped. Just like that. I wasn't sure what to do . . . though checking to see if someone was flying this thing sounded like a pretty good place to start. So did talking the pilot into turning around and getting me back home before Mom and Dad found out I was missing.

I reached up to the floor panel above my face and gave it a shove. It seemed to weigh a lot less than I remembered. The reason was simple. It did weigh a lot less. In fact, it weighed absolutely nothing! I let it go and watched as it just floated . . . right along with my hand, my arm, and my whole body!

Talk about cool. It was like swimming, but without all the bother of having to put on sunscreen, or getting your hair wet, or drowning.

With no effort at all, I pulled myself through the opening and up onto the mid deck. Wow. This weightlessness stuff was incredible. The slightest push and you'd go on forever. That explains why I suddenly shot across the mid deck at a hundred miles an hour, banged my head against the front wall,

Ooaf!

and started to see stars that had nothing to do with being in outer space.

When my head cleared, I noticed I was floating upside down. Of course, I panicked, grabbed the nearest wall, and flipped myself around. But I didn't know the strength of my own flip. Suddenly I spun head over heels, around and around, and then around some more . . . until I crashed into the same wall again.

Ooaf!

After a couple more constellations drifted past my vision, I carefully steadied myself. Then, slowly, cautiously, I let go and just let myself drift. It was fantastic! The only problem was that all the acrobatics and weightlessness had made my stomach a little restless. It wasn't that I was sick or anything, it's just that the food inside my stomach kept wanting to get outside to see what was going on. I did a pretty good job of holding it down. And

I figured if that was my only problem, things wouldn't be so bad.

Then I turned and saw the two astronauts strapped into the chairs at the back wall and realized things were worse than bad.

They sat there staring at me, with their mouths hanging open. The old days of space suits and stuff were long gone. Now they just wore what looked like crash helmets and blue overalls with a bunch of zippers and pockets.

I gave kind of a weak smile. Then a weaker wave. Then squeaked out an even weaker, "Hi."

They just kept staring.

I cleared my throat and tried to sound calm and casual. I might have pulled it off if my voice weren't high and quivering. I sounded like a Vienna Choir Boy sitting on a blender. "I, uh, I think I kind of got separated from my tour group."

They looked at each other and then back to me.

"Um . . ." my stomach was getting more and more queasy. Any minute now I was afraid we'd be playing a very gross version of show and tell. "Listen, uh, you don't happen to know where I could find, um, a bathroom, do you?"

The one to the left, a woman, pointed toward a little compartment drawer nearby. It was labeled "Space Sickness Bags." I nodded gratefully and pushed toward it as fast as I could . . . which meant another collision with another wall.

Ooaf! (This was getting to be a habit.)

Meanwhile, I heard the woman's voice speaking into her intercom. "Uh, Skipper, we have a little situation down here."

* * * * *

Several minutes (and two full space sickness bags) later, all five of us were meeting on the mid deck. Nobody seemed too thrilled about my being there, but luckily, it didn't look like they were going to make me get out and walk home. Their names were:

COMMANDER PHILLIPS: He was in charge of the mission. I immediately liked him, especially when he decided not to throw me overboard.

PILOT O'BRIEN: I wasn't crazy about him, especially when he kept saying they should throw me overboard.

MISSION SPECIALIST DR. LAMBERT: The woman who introduced me to my new hobby of collecting (and filling) space sickness bags.

PAYLOAD SPECIALIST MEYER: A practical joker with a mischievous twinkle. If they gave space swirlies, noogies, or wedgies, he'd be the guy to look out for.

"The way I see it," Commander Phillips was saying, "we can either abort the mission and head home . . . or continue with some minor adjustments."

"If we abort," Pilot O'Brien frowned, "we won't be able to deliver the next section of the space station. It'll postpone the station's whole assembly schedule . . . by months."

Commander Phillips nodded.

"And we won't be able to replenish the supplies of the crew that's up in the station now," Meyer said.

"Or test the Personal Rescue Enclosures," Dr. Lambert added. "That's a major exercise we had scheduled."

Commander Phillips turned to me and sighed. "Your little stunt could cost NASA a bundle."

I swallowed and croaked, "I mow a lot of lawns during the summer."

"Son, at the cost of this mission, you'd be mowing lawns until the year 2275."

"I also do gardening."

The crew chuckled, everyone but Pilot O'Brien,

who seemed to be looking from me to the exit hatch a lot. I wasn't sure what he had in mind, but just to be safe, I inched a little closer to Commander Phillips.

"What does Houston say?" Dr. Lambert asked as she handed me another space sickness bag.

"Control says it's our call," Commander Phillips answered.

O'Brien turned to me and scowled. "What do you say, Willy?"

"Uh, my name's Wally."

"Whatever."

"I'd, uh, be happy to stay," I said. "But don't I need a note from home or something?" I gave a nervous little laugh.

No one laughed back.

O'Brien glanced at his watch and grumbled. "We've got an OMS burn coming up. We better make a decision."

"Check with Control again," Commander Phillips ordered. "See if you can get his parents."

O'Brien nodded and pushed up toward the flight deck. "Come on, Wilbur," he ordered.

"Uh, that's Wally," I said.

"Whatever."

I threw a nervous glance to Commander Phillips who nodded that I should follow.

"I don't think he likes you," Meyer whispered.

"Are there any exit hatches up on the flight deck?" I whispered back.

Meyer grinned and shook his head. "But if I were you, I wouldn't go sitting in any ejection seats."

I gave a weak smile and pushed off toward the flight deck. I would have performed an encore of my famous crash-and-burn routine, but Dr. Lambert reached out and caught me.

"Easy," she said, steadying me. "Not so fast."

"Thanks."

"You certainly have your share of accidents, don't you?"

If you only knew, I thought.

"Willard!" Captain O'Brien called from flight deck. "Get up here!"

I drifted through the opening and up onto the flight deck. Suddenly I sucked in my breath. It was awesome. The Earth, I mean. It filled all the windows and it was absolutely breathtaking. I know we've seen hundreds of pictures of it in hundreds of books and videos, but nothing even came close to capturing its real beauty . . . all the blues and greens from the ocean, the darker greens and golds from the land. And, of course, all the glowing white clouds swirling across its surface. I tell you, God must get a lot of compliments with something like this hanging in his living room.

O'Brien crawled into the pilot's seat. "That's the island of Madagascar down there."

I nodded in quiet awe. Not being a geography guy I didn't know Madagascar from Montana, but it didn't matter. The view was incredible. I swallowed and tried to say what I was thinking, "It's . . . so . . . so . . ."

"Yeah," he nodded quietly, "you took the words right out of my mouth." He pressed a button and checked a monitor. "We're 145 miles high." He pressed another button and continued, "and we're traveling almost 25 times the speed of sound."

He reached for a small headset with a microphone and earpiece. "Here," he said, handing it to me, "put this on."

A few seconds later we were talking with Earth.

"Roger, *Encounter*," a voice in the headset answered. "We have the boy's father waiting on line in Florida. We are patching you in now."

There was a crackle, some static, and then:

"Hello? . . . Wally? Wally are you there?"

I recognized the voice instantly. It had that wonderful mixture of love, anger, and concern.

"Hi, Dad," I said.

"Well, you've really, really done it this time, haven't you, son?"

"I guess I have."

"I mean you've really, *really* done it."

"Yes, I really have."

"I mean really, really, real—"

"Dad?"

"Yes, son?"

"This is really, really long distance, so we better get on with it."

"Oh, yes, good point." He cleared his throat. "The people at NASA want to know if you should come down or if they can continue the mission."

"What did you say?" I asked.

"I said I needed to talk to you. Now, they assure me it's just as safe whether you stay a couple of days in orbit or come back right away. I have no reason to doubt them, but if you're uncomfortable with staying up there and want to come back down—"

"No, Dad, I really like it up here."

"I mean it, son, just say the word, and I'll have them bring you back right now, this very—"

"No, Dad, really."

"Are you sure?"

"You bet," I said, grabbing a pencil that was drifting by. I gave it a spin and watched it twirl across the cabin. "It's really cool. What does Mom say?"

"Well, she's pretty nervous, especially the thought of you being up there all that time without any clean underwear."

I smiled. "Any other messages?"

"Just Wall Street. She's already made some deal with a Hollywood studio. They want to make sure you do lots of your usual crazy McDoogle stuff so they'll have enough material for a movie and maybe a sequel."

I forced a chuckle.

So did Dad, but I could tell he was holding back his real feelings. "Dad?"

"Yes, son."

"Tell me what you think. *Really,* I mean."

"I uh . . . well, that is to say . . ."

I felt a lump growing in my throat. Good ol' Dad. He always had trouble talking about his emotions.

"I, uh . . . "

"Go ahead Dad, you can tell me." On good days, when we're alone, he can sometimes express his feelings. On bad days, when he thinks people are listening, he covers up by going for something macho like dollars and cents.

"Well . . . right now NASA's picking up the bill for all of our food and lodging. But if we cancel the mission, they said I'm going to have to pay for everything."

Good ol' Dad. By the sound of things, there must have been a thousand people in the room listening to him.

"Well, okay then," I said. "That makes the choice even easier. We better go for it."

Chapter 4

Another Day, Another Catastrophe

Commander Phillips and Pilot O'Brien were up on the flight deck getting ready for what was called an "OMS burn" . . . or for you civilian types, that's *Orbital Maneuvering System* burn. Impressed? Me, too. But, I'd be even more impressed if I knew how to use their bathroom. I'm sure they had one. And, after all this time inside the shuttle, I needed to use it . . . bad. Unfortunately, the idea of using a toilet without any gravity was scarier than not using any at all. So I waited.

Down below, on the mid deck, Payload Specialist Meyer was explaining the OMS burn to me. "We're scheduled to rendezvous with the crew of the space station. They're at a 200-mile orbit, so we have to fire our engines and accelerate to rise to their altitude."

I nodded, pretending to understand what he

was talking about. But, at the moment, I was more concerned about getting into the package of juice Dr. Lambert had given me to help calm my stomach.

"It's not that difficult," she chuckled. "It's almost like the juice cartons on Earth. All you do is insert this little straw here into that little hole there."

Unfortunately, that sounded a lot like physical coordination which, as we've already established, is not one of my specialties.

Suddenly, Commander Phillips' voice came over our headsets: "Okay, everybody, stand by for OMS burn."

I continued struggling with the straw.

"Uh, Wally," Meyer motioned toward one of the portable footholds that they'd placed all around the cabin. "You'll want to slip your foot into that."

I appreciated the thought, but by now I was a pro at being weightless. No way would I go flying across the cabin just by putting a little straw into a little hole.

Commander Phillips' voice continued: "And, five, four, three . . ."

"Wally," Meyer motioned urgently to the foothold.

I nodded politely as I kept fighting to get the straw into the hole.

". . . two, one . . ."

There was a loud WHOMP as the engines fired. The sudden acceleration sent me sailing across the cabin. *Oh no,* I thought, *here we go again.* But this crash-and-burn routine had a brand new twist . . . the bag of juice in my hand. The bag of juice that hit the wall just before I hit it. The bag of juice that I squashed flat, squirting a gusher of Papaya Delight out of the hole and all over myself.

That was the good news. The bad news was that it didn't fall to the floor or soak into my lap. Instead, it just floated all around the mid deck in little juice balls.

"Get it!" Meyer shouted as he unhooked his feet and shoved off in my direction. "Slurp it up before it gets into the electrical equipment!"

I immediately obeyed. So did Dr. Lambert. Soon all three of us were darting around the cabin slurping little balls of juice into our mouths. We looked like dolphins or seals the way we swam and dipped and bobbed. Come to think of it, we sounded like them, too, the way we slurped and laughed and giggled.

It was pretty funny . . . except for the part when it got into your hair, or splattered all over your body, or when Pilot O'Brien came down from the flight deck to see what all the commotion was about.

"What's going on?" he barked. "Who's responsible?"

All eyes shifted to me. I tried to give him my politest smile and most respectful attention. I would have pulled it off, too, if it weren't for the loud belch that suddenly slipped out.

"What is the meaning of this? What do you have to say for yourself?"

All of the bouncing and drinking and jiggling had taken its toll. I definitely had something to say, though it wasn't exactly what he expected. I opened my mouth and in my calmest, most mature voice screamed, "If I don't go to the bathroom, I'm going to explode!"

In one quick move O'Brien shoved off, grabbed me by the shoulder, and pushed us toward the exit hatch.

"No!" I cried. "I'm only kidding, I can wait, I can wait!"

To my relief he was not throwing me outside. He was taking me to the Waste Collection System which was just to the left of the hatch.

In a second he had placed my feet in some metal footholds so I wouldn't float. Next, he seatbelted me onto what almost looked like an airline's toilet seat, snapped on what almost sounded like a giant vacuum cleaner, and pointed to what almost looked like a giant vacuum cleaner hose . . . except for the giant opening. I'll save you the details, but if you understand the principal of suction and that the giant vacuum cleaner hose really did work like a giant vacuum cleaner hose . . .well, then you sort of get the idea of how to use a bathroom in outer space.

Fortunately, washing my hands came a little easier. Across the way was a clear plastic bubble with a couple of hand holes in it. All you had to do was turn on the water and shove your hands inside the bubble. It would shoot water out of one side, spray it all over your hands, and suck the used water out the other side.

It was pretty cool the way they kept using suction to replace gravity. Still, I wasn't looking forward to taking any showers.

* * * * *

"Hey, Wally," Meyer called from the flight deck. "Come up here. You'll want to see this!"

I drifted through the opening where O'Brien and Meyer were both standing. But instead of facing forward, they were facing backwards. They had their hands on a bunch of controls as they stared through two rear windows that looked out into the cargo bay. The cargo bay doors had been opened several hours earlier, and there was a huge cylinder-like tank inside. The cylinder was going to be a new section on the space station we were headed to."

Take a look," Meyer said as he pointed to the right window.

Outside, off to the right, was the space station. I'd seen pictures of it on TV, but not up close and in person. It was pretty cool. There were lots of framework girders and solar panels and stuff. There were also three or four of those giant cylinders exactly like the one we were about to unload.

A new voice came through the intercom. "You're looking good, *Encounter*."

Pilot O'Brien pressed a button and answered, "Roger. We're standing by and waiting for your word to commence RMS."

"Who're you talking to?" I asked.

"Someone in the space station," Meyer said, as he flipped a few switches. "There are six of them. They've been up here a little over two months."

I looked back up to the station. It seemed weird that there were six human beings actually living inside that thing. Weirder still was that they actually wanted to live there. I mean, for a home it wasn't much to look at (though I guess you wouldn't have problems with noisy neighbors or door-to-door salesmen). Also, there wasn't a lot of grass to mow, weeds to pull, or leaves to rake. And if they got cable, well, maybe living up there wouldn't be such a bad deal, after all—unless, of course, you were the one who had to empty the catbox . . . or walk the dog.

"What's that?" I asked, pointing to a long, fifty-foot pole stretched out above the cargo bay.

"That's the remote manipulator," Meyer said. "It's like a giant arm that allows me to pick things up and move them around from inside here."

I looked at the controls he had his hands on. One was above and between the two windows, the other was lower and to the right. They looked exactly like joysticks from some computer game, except probably a couple million dollars more expensive.

"Want to see how it works?" Meyer asked.

"Sure!"

"Give me your hands."

"You think that's such a good idea?" O'Brien frowned as he worked his own set of controls beside us.

"There's nothing we can do but wait until they give us the word. What can the kid hurt?"

Part of me wanted to explain that I could hurt plenty. After all we are talking Wally If-It-Can-Mess-Up-Crack-Up-Or-Blow-Up-It-Will McDoogle. But the other part of me really wanted the chance to play astronaut. Unfortunately, that was the part that won out.

Carefully putting my hands on the controls and resting his on top of mine, Meyer explained what each button and each movement did. It wasn't too complicated, and after a while I actually started to get the hang of it. Finally he removed his hands and let me hold the controls by myself.

What a rush! I was sweating, my heart was pounding, and my hands were shaking.

"Okay," he smiled. Now just do everything I tell you . . . *very, very* slowly."

I nodded.

"And whatever you do, never, *never* press that button."

"This button here?" I asked, accidentally bumping into it. Suddenly the arm spun to the left and crashed into the side of our payload.

THUD.

The entire craft gave a shudder.

"Yup," Meyer groaned, "that was the one."

We all stared out the window. Everything looked in pretty good shape. Well, except for the giant dent I had just put in the cylinder. Too bad. To travel all this way just to deliver damaged merchandise.

I could feel O'Brien's eyes boring into me. After more silence than I thought was necessary, I cleared my throat and said, "Boy, I hope they won't ask for a discount." I gave them a sick look and forced a smile.

They returned the sick look. They did not return the smile.

Chapter 5

~~Sweet~~ Sweat Dreams

It was hard for me to get to sleep that night.

The lights were dimmed, and we were all inside our blue sleeping bags that were strapped to boards so we wouldn't float around. Of course, that didn't do much to hold down our arms or hair. It was kinda spooky looking around and seeing everybody's arms raised out like zombies' and their hair floating around like some Albert Einstein picture.

But not as spooky as Meyer's snoring. While everyone was cutting Z's, it sounded like he was cutting down an entire rain forest . . . with about a hundred chain saws . . . all at once. But it wasn't the floating arms, or hair, or Meyer's snoring that kept me awake.

It was my thoughts about a pattern that had been forming. It seemed every time I broke the slightest rule, disaster hit.

—I sneak a little drink into Launch Control . . .
and I wind up getting Ms. Durkelbuster fired.

—I slip on my glasses and step into the shuttle . . .
and I wind up as an afterthought astronaut.

—I press one little button . . .
and I practically destroy a space station.

Now, I'm no genius or anything, but it started to look like maybe God was trying to tell me something . . . and it wasn't who was going to win next year's World Series. It was something about rules and about following them. Call me crazy, but I was getting the feeling He expected me to follow *all* the rules, no matter how small or stupid they may seem.

But, at the moment I wasn't in the mood for a Sunday school lesson, so I tried to drown out those thoughts by reaching for ol' Betsy and seeing what Neutron Dude was up to. . . .

When we last left our nuclear good guy, he was about to zap across the phone wires to find the notoriously nutsoid, and sickeningly healthy... Veggie-Man.

Neutron Dude races through the telephone wires and leaps out of the receiver only to discover...

Leapin' Lima beans! Great granola bars! Holy whole grain! (I've got more, but I'll save them for later.) It's worse than he had expected. Everywhere he looks there are organically-grown vegetables, piles and piles of boiled beets, rows and rows of steamed spinach. Such wholesome wholeness is more than our hero (and part-time junk food junkie) can take. He is overwhelmed. He starts to stagger, to overreact, to have a meltdown.

Then, suddenly, the laboratory doors open and in rolls a giant truckload of his favorite Chewy-Gooey Bars. Neutron Dude glows in relief. At least he won't starve. At least he'll have something to snack on between all that nauseating no-fatness.

But, great green beans! (I told you I had more.) Holy hicjama! (Trust me, it's a vegetable.) Odious okra! (So's that.) They're not unloading beautiful, caramel-covered Chewy Gooies...they're unloading ta-da-Daa)caramel-covered squash! Our hero shudders at the thought of finding one of those in his lunchbox.

Suddenly he hears a voice.

"Welcome, Atom Brain."

Neutron Dude spins around. It's Veggie-Man. The superhero can tell by the smell of overcooked cabbage and the green color of Veggie-Man's face caused by one too many cucumbers on his breakfast cereal. In his hand he holds the dreaded can of Health Food Spray. The dreaded spray that is turning all the world's food into health food.

"Give it up!" Neutron Dude crackles. "In the name of all that is edible and tasty, turn yourself in."

Veggie-Man sneers his best bad guy sneer. "I've not even begun. You think it's just food I'm turning into fruits and vegetables? No way. It's everything." He points and sprays the can at one of his assistants, a plump, red-faced man, who suddenly becomes a plump, ruby-red tomato.

Neutron Dude gasps a good guy gasp.

Veggie-Man laughs a menacing laugh. "I'm turning everything into wholesomeness. People, mountains, freeways, rivers. Even as we speak, my formula is being released into all of the waters of the world."

"You don't mean..."

"That's right. Instead of water skiing, you'll be vegetable-soup skiing."

"And fishing?"

"Trout will become diced carrots. Tuna, chopped celery. Shrimp will be—"

"You can't do this!" Neutron-Dude shouts.

"Oh, but I already am." He aims his deadly Health Spray directly at our good guy. "And you, Neutron Numbskull. What will it be? A giant green bean? Parsley? How would you like to become a nice turnip?"

Suddenly Neutron Dude knows what he has to do, so he does what he has to do, and he does it brilliantly. (Or something like that.) He points his Proton Belt, adjusts the setting to "Deep Fry," and fires a bolt of supercharged microwaves at the villainous villain.

But Veggie-Man is too fast. He sprays the microwaves with his formula, and the bolt of energy drops to the floor transformed into a giant French fry.

Neutron Dude tries again.

The next bolt falls as a fried zucchini.

And again.

Now we're talking an overcooked pickle.

Veggie-Man chuckles a creepy chuckle. "It's all over, Neutron Dude." Again he points the can at our hero. "Now it's time for *you* to be whole-heartedly healthy."

His finger presses down on the nozzle, but just before the spray shoots out—"

"Hey, Wendell!" It was Pilot O'Brien. "Shut that thing off and get some sleep. We've got a big day tomorrow, and we'll need your help."

I looked across to his sleeping bag. The guy wasn't smiling. But at least, for once, he wasn't scowling. Was it my imagination, or was O'Brien actually warming up to me?

"Shut it down, Wing nut," he barked. "That's an order."

Well, so much for warming up. I nodded and turned ol' Betsy off. But as I snuggled deeper into my bag, I couldn't help wondering exactly what he meant by needing my help.

Unfortunately, I'd soon find out. . . .

* * * * *

The following morning I had some cereal and grape juice (this time without chasing little balls all over the cabin). I also used the bathroom (this time without panicking over giant vacuum cleaner nozzles.) I tell you, I was becoming a real pro with this weightlessness stuff. I even managed to brush my teeth without a major problem . . . although the rinsing and spitting got kind of tricky.

Eventually, I joined the rest of the crew on the mid deck where they were having a discussion. It felt pretty cool being part of an official NASA meeting. It would have felt cooler if I weren't the reason for that meeting.

"So, Control doesn't want us to deliver that section of space station?" O'Brien frowned.

Commander Phillips nodded. "We need to take it back home, check it out, and send it up on the next mission."

There was a long silence. My stomach was feeling kind of queasy, but it had nothing to do with space sickness.

"Don't feel bad," Commander Phillips said to me. "Anybody could have damaged that seven million dollar section of brand new, space station."

I nodded, but for some reason felt no better.

"Well," he hesitated, "almost anybody."

I nodded again, feeling even worse.

"Well, actually, come to think of it, it's supposed to be foolproof, but foolproof is not the same as, . . . well you know."

I finished the thought for him, "Foolproof is not the same as McDoogle-proof ?"

He grinned, grateful that I'd caught the drift.

"What about the manipulator arm?" O'Brien scowled. "Is that damaged, too?"

Payload Specialist Meyer shook his head. "It's in pretty good shape, although it sticks in a couple of places."

Dr. Lambert was the next to speak. "Can we still proceed with the Emergency Evacuation Exercise?"

Meyer nodded. "As long as Wally stays on board, where he can do no more harm."

Everyone agreed, including me.

"He can have my spacesuit during the evacuation." Commander Phillips said. "I'll use one of the extra rescue balls."

"*Evacuation?*" I nervously squawked. No one answered. I tried again, a little louder. "*Spacesuit?*" And again. "*Rescue balls?*"

"Relax," Meyer grinned. "We'll be leaving, but you'll be staying right here."

"I will?" I asked in relief, as I felt my heart rate drop back to 200.

"Absolutely," he said. "We'll be doing the exercise, but you and O'Brien will stay behind, just the two of you, all by yourselves. You'll be perfectly safe."

My heart leaped back into Hyper-beat. I threw a nervous look to O'Brien. But before I could ask Meyer to give me his exact definition of *safe*, O'Brien turned to me and growled, "Let's get suited up, Weldon."

"That's Wally."

"Whatever."

"Where are we going?"

He pointed to a large round hatch at the back of the mid deck. "Into the airlock."

"Airlock?" I cried. "Aren't airlocks what you go through before you go out into outer space?"

"That's right." He pushed off to the hatch, reached for the lever, gave it a pull, and slid it open. There was a slight hiss. He turned to me, and for the first time since I'd met him, there was a smile on his lips. Or was it a sneer? "Let's go."

I swallowed, said a prayer, and promised God I'd never, never break another rule as long as I lived. Of course, He'd have to let me live a little longer to prove it. Unfortunately, I couldn't tell if He was in the mood for making that kind of deal or not. . . .

Chapter 6

Batter Up!

Getting into the space suit, or the *Extravehicular Mobility Unit* (see how educational this is becoming?) wasn't as tough as I thought. The hardest part was standing there for a few minutes longer than forever, just breathing through some sort of face mask.

"It cleans the nitrogen out of your blood," O'Brien explained.

"That's good," I said, once again having no idea what he was talking about.

Finally, he handed me something like a pair of long johns that had a bunch of little tubes running all through it.

"Oh boy," I said, "spaghetti underwear."

"Slip it on," he ordered. "Those little tubes carry water to help keep your body cool."

Next came the bottom half of the actual space

suit. It was pretty stiff and bulky, and it had little straps inside to adjust it to my height. Since I'm not exactly your most full-grown astronaut I had to cinch those straps up tight. But, other than that, there were no problems . . . until I looked down to where my toes should be and only saw my heels. "My feet are on backwards!" I cried.

O'Brien looked up from his own suit and sighed. "It's not your feet, Wilbur, It's your suit. You got into it backwards."

"Oh," I laughed nervously, "Right. I knew that." I quickly turned around and tried again.

Next came the top half of the suit. Like the bottom half, it was also pretty bulky. And, like the bottom half, there were only two ways of putting it on. So after putting it on the wrong way (what else is new), I turned around and got into it the right way.

Next came the gloves. Two ways, two tries. This was getting monotonous.

A moment later O'Brien floated over to me. "On your chest here is a little computer readout. It tells you how much oxygen you have left and how strong your battery is. These suits are good for seven hours, so we'll have plenty of time for the exercise."

"Exactly what exercise are we talking about?" I asked.

"We're staging an emergency drill on the

shuttle. Space is a complete vacuum, so first we'll depressurize the cabin. Next we'll transport the crew from in there," he pointed to the mid deck, "to a cable out there," he pointed toward the hatch leading outside.

"Not me," I cried, "I'm not going out there!" It really wasn't a statement, more like a pleading and begging for my life. It's not that I'm afraid of outer space, it's just that heights make me nervous. And being 200 miles above the earth is definitely on the high side of heights.

"Don't worry," O'Brien said. "You will be inside the shuttle the whole time—up on the flight deck."

A wave of relief washed over me. "What about you?" I asked.

"Once I hook the others to the cable line connecting the shuttle to the station, I'll come in to join you."

More waves, more relief.

O'Brien grabbed something like a cap and slipped it over my head. It had headphones that fit over my ears and little microphones on both sides of my mouth.

Finally came the helmet. It was pretty neat, like putting your head inside a fish bowl. Though I wouldn't try that at home, especially if it still happens to have water or fish inside.

Now I heard O'Brien speaking through my headset. "Do you hear me?" he asked.

I nodded.

"Good. O'Brien to Commander Phillips. How are you coming in there, Skipper?"

Commander Phillips answered. "Everyone's set. Meyer has attached the cable to the space station, and I'm getting into the final ball now."

"Roger, we're on our way." O'Brien turned and headed back through the hatch to the mid deck. I followed. But, instead of meeting our three astronaut buddies, we were met by three giant balls, each about a yard wide.

"Where'd they go?" I asked.

"Take a peek," O'Brien said, motioning to a tiny little porthole inside the nearest ball.

I floated over to the ball and looked inside. To my surprise I saw Dr. Lambert sitting in there, all scrunched up and breathing air through a mask. She looked up and waved.

I waved back and moved to the next ball where I saw Commander Phillips. Call me a genius, but when I got to the third ball I had a sneaking suspicion I'd see Meyer. I was right.

"They're called Personal Rescue Enclosures," O'Brien explained through my headset. "They're like miniature space suits, and they have enough oxygen inside to last an hour."

Before I could ask any more questions, another voice came through my headset. "Shuttle *Encounter*, this is Space Station One. We've got plenty of milk and cookies waiting. Are you folks about ready to drop by for a visit?"

Commander Phillips answered over the radio from inside his ball. "We're packaged, sealed, and ready for delivery."

O'Brien turned to me. "Okay, Warren—"

"Wally," I corrected.

"Whatever. I'm going to depressurize the cabin and open up the airlock. Go on up to the flight deck and for goodness' sake, don't touch anything!"

I didn't have to be told twice. I turned and floated up toward the flight deck. Before I arrived, I heard a loud hiss. O'Brien was opening the hatch. I could feel my suit balloon out as the pressure inside pushed against the vacuum that was filling the shuttle.

Once up on the flight deck I floated over to the back cargo bay windows to watch. A line was stretched from our airlock hatch all the way to Space Station One. O'Brien had just opened our hatch and appeared with one of the balls. He lifted it and somehow attached it to the line. It must have been Meyer because through the intercom I heard, "Looks like I'm really being hung out to dry."

The others chuckled as the next ball was attached. And then the last.

There were lots of wisecracks back and forth as if this were something they did every day. But I could tell they were a little bit nervous. When O'Brien finished, he disappeared back into the shuttle. A moment later he floated up onto the flight deck beside me and took hold of the controls of the manipulator arm.

"Space Station One," he said, "this is *Encounter*. I'm delivering the packages now."

"Roger," came the reply.

O'Brien expertly moved the manipulator arm to the space balls hanging from the cable. Then, ever-so-gently, he nudged them down the line toward the space station. I watched as he carefully worked the controls. It seemed to take forever, but the guy was taking no chances.

At last the rescue balls reached the space station.

"Space Station One," O'Brien said. "Your mail is in."

"Copy," the voice replied. "Let's see what we've got."

I could see the hatch to the space station open. It was an air lock exactly like ours. One of their guys in a suit exactly like ours appeared. He looked over and gave us a wave. Next he grabbed the three balls and pulled each of them inside.

Finally, he turned back to us, gave another wave, climbed into his airlock, and shut the door.

"Nice work," came the voice from the space station. "Mission accomplished."

Well, not quite . . .

Pilot O'Brien took the controls and started to move the manipulator arm back to our shuttle but nothing happened. It was stuck, just as Meyer had earlier mentioned (thanks to my little handiwork from the day before). O'Brien pushed harder. Still nothing. He pushed the other way. Repeat performance.

I looked on amazed. Another McDoogle mishap was taking place before my very eyes, and I wasn't touching a thing! Am I getting good, or what?

O'Brien pushed even harder. Still no action. Then, suddenly, the arm jerked free. That was the good news. The bad news was it jerked free and slammed into the side of the space station hatch.

K-BAMB

The entire space station shook. So did the shuttle.

Someone from the space station called, "Easy, big fellow, easy."

"Sorry," O'Brien said, trying to sound casual and

nonchalant. But I could tell that he was really worried. "Uh, Space Station One, could you give that hatch of yours a try? Check to see if it still opens."

"Say again?"

"I banged your hatch pretty hard. I just want to verify that it's still operational."

"Roger."

There was a long moment of silence as we watched and waited. With any luck everything would be okay. With any luck there would be no more problems from my little accident yesterday.

Then again, we all know about McDoogle and luck, don't we?

At last, we heard a voice over our headsets. "No go at this end. Looks like we might have ourselves a situation."

No one answered.

I could tell they were all thinking. The jokes and chatter had suddenly stopped. There was only silence.

The next voice was Commander Phillips'. "O'Brien. You'll have to come over and try to open it from the outside."

O'Brien threw me a look. "That would mean leaving Walden all alone in the shuttle."

My mouth suddenly went dry. Not, I-don't-have-anything-to-swallow dry, but dry-as-a-cotton-ball-in-the-Sahara-desert-in-the-middle-of-a-heat-wave dry. "Can't . . ." my voice caught. I cleared it and started again. "Can't they go out another door and fix it themselves?"

"That's their only door," O'Brien said. "If we don't open it, they'll never get out."

"What type of idiot would build a space station with only one door?" I asked in amazement. "There should be another section with another door."

"There is," O'Brien said grimly. He pointed to the new section still sitting in our cargo bay. The new section that I had ruined by putting a giant dent in it. "It's right there. . . ."

* * * * *

Ten minutes passed. Everyone went over the problem again and again, and then again some more. Each time they came to the same solution: Pilot O'Brien would have to cross over and free up the hatch handle from the outside. It wasn't anyone's favorite solution, but since it was the only one we had, they decided to go for it.

I watched through the cargo bay window as Pilot O'Brien reopened our outside airlock. Next, he attached a short cable from his suit to the "clothesline" that ran from the shuttle to the space station.

"I've attached my tether," he said over the radio. "I'm pushing off now."

"Be careful," Commander Phillips warned.

He made his way slowly across the line toward the space station. I don't know why I was so nervous. Maybe it was being all alone in the shuttle. Maybe it was O'Brien being out there all by himself. Or maybe it was knowing that, thanks to me, the door to the space station was jammed shut. Thanks to me, all six members of the station as well as Commander Phillips, Dr. Lambert, and Meyer were trapped inside. It's not that I'm the nervous type or anything, but being responsible for the life (or death) of nine people can put you a little on edge.

Then, to top it off, I started to do what I always do when I'm nervous. I started to itch. The itches on my arms and legs weren't so bad. I could reach them.

But then my nose started to itch.

Now, on Earth it's no big deal. When your nose itches, all you have to do is reach up and give the ol' honker a scratch. But it's not quite so easy in outer space when you're wearing a space helmet. Think about it. How do you scratch your nose when you're inside a space helmet?

I had no answer, and I was needing one more and more desperately. I had to do something. I gave my head a little shake, hoping it would help.

It made the itch worse.

I tried again. Nothing.

And again, even harder.

More of nothing.

Something had to be done. By now it was unbearable. I tried not to think about it. But the more I thought about not thinking about it, the more I was thinking about thinking about it, which made it even worse.

I shook my head, this time for all I was worth. The good news was my glasses slipped half way off my nose and hit the itch dead center.

All right! Score!

The bad news was my glasses now set cockeyed on my face. *Majorly* cockeyed. So cockeyed that I could no longer see out of them—well except for one tiny left-hand corner at the bottom.

But that was okay. It's not like I had to do anything or see anything. All I had to do is sit still until they all got back. Just sit still, and as O'Brien had said, "don't touch a thing."

No problem.

"William?" O'Brien's voice came though my headset. "I'm going to need your help."

Now we had a problem.

I looked back out the window to O'Brien. It took a little doing, holding my head just right to catch a glimpse of him through the bottom corner of my left lens. I noticed that his tether was too short and that he had unhooked it to reach the hatch. But that was okay, he had a good firm hold on the hatch handle and wasn't going anywhere.

"William," he said again, "the manipulator arm is blocking the door. I'm going to need you to move it just a few inches to the left."

"Me?" It was supposed to be a question. It came out like a scream.

"Relax, it's not that difficult. I know you watched me maneuver the arm into position, and I know Meyer showed you how to use it yesterday."

"Yeah, but . . ."

"Just take the Rational Hand Controller and—"

"The what?"

"The handle to the right and below the window. Just push it, *ever so slowly,* to the left."

Commander Phillips' voice came over the radio. "Are you sure that's such a good idea?"

"Yeah," I squeaked, "remember what happened the last time I helped."

"It's a simple procedure," O'Brien insisted. "Just push the handle to the left, *very* slowly and *very* slightly."

I waited for somebody else to butt in, for somebody to explain to him who he was dealing with. But nobody said a word . . .

Except O'Brien. "Let's go, Walden!"

I was trapped. There was no way out. Oh, sure, I could mention my cockeyed glasses and that I couldn't see a thing. But he'd already seen my stupendous coordination for the past twenty-four hours. And if that didn't scare him off, then the minor problem of being totally blind wouldn't do the trick either.

With a deep breath I slowly reached for the handle. My heart pounded like a rap song gone berserk as I inched my hand closer and closer. So far, so good. Well, except for the part where my glasses were so far off my face that I couldn't judge the distance.

When I thought I had a good six inches to go before I touched the handle, my hand bumped into it. Not much, but enough.

"WHAT ARE YOU DOING? *WADSWORTH?* . . ."

I looked up just in time to see the manipulator arm smack into O'Brien. Not very hard, but enough.

"*W A D S W O R T H* . . ."

He had nothing to hang onto. Nothing to catch himself with. He started to sail away, in slow-motion. His arms and legs began to flail, like he was swimming, digging in all directions at once.

But nothing he did helped. There was nothing he could do to stop himself as he slowly drifted away from the space station. Even though my glasses were cockeyed, I still managed to see the look on his face. And I still wished I hadn't. It made my blood run cold. It was the look of sheer terror—the same terror that filled his voice as he slowly sailed past my window and out into space.

"*HELP ME!* . . ."

Chapter 7

Rescue

"Wally, Wally, listen to me very carefully." It was Commander Phillips. He was still over at the space station. By the sound of things, he'd crawled out of his little ball and was looking through one of their windows. "O'Brien needs your help."

"What do we do?" I cried.

"I'm afraid it's not *we* Wally. There's nothing *we* can do. We're all locked up inside here."

"Then who?" I asked, already feeling a tiny ball knotting in my stomach.

"I'm afraid it's *you*."

"Me?" That tiny ball in my stomach had just become a beach ball.

"You're the only one who can help. If you don't get out there and grab him, if you don't bring him back, O'Brien will be floating in space forever."

"He can't float there forever," I said looking down to the digital readout on my chest. Since my glasses were still cockeyed, it took a little neck twisting and craning to finally make out the numbers. "He's only got 6.1 hours of air left."

"Then you better get moving."

I'll save you the ugly details . . .

—Like how I begged and pleaded for them to find another way.
—How I whimpered and whined about my fear of heights.
—How I blubbered and bawled (not a good idea unless you like watching little tear drops floating around inside your space helmet) for them to find another hero.

Nothing worked. They were fresh out of heroes. In fact, they were fresh out of humans. All they had was me.

And then I heard it: O'Brien's voice. It was weak and very, very frightened. ". . . Wendell . . . help me . . . please . . ."

All of my life I'd played the superhero, but only in my writing. Only on my laptop, where all that could go wrong was getting a good case of writer's cramp. But now, . . . now the only thing that could go wrong was . . . well, just about everything. The possibilities were mind-boggling! The chances of chaos, staggering.

". . . Please, Willard . . ."

But what other choice did I have? I knew I'd probably botch things up. I knew I'd probably die a couple dozen times in the process. But somebody had to do something. And since I was the only somebody around, I knew I was elected.

Five minutes later I stood inside the air hatch as Commander Phillips gave me careful directions. "Find the switch labeled: AIRLOCK DEPRESS."

I tilted my head and squinted until I saw it through my bottom left lens. "Got it."

"Is it turned to '0' POSITION?"

More tilting and more squinting. "Yes."

"Good. Then reach up, pull the handle, and slide open the hatch."

I did. And what I saw (or sort of saw) took my breath away. Directly below me was the Earth. But not the Earth through a space shuttle window. This was the earth with nothing between us but 200 miles of nothing.

I gasped.

"Sounds like you're outside," Commander Phillips chuckled.

I tried to answer, but that would mean having to catch my breath. And right now it was a little lost in all the fear and in all the beauty.

"Wally, are you there? Wally? Wally!"

"Present," I croaked.

"We're going to have to hurry. Every second we waste, O'Brien drifts farther from the shuttle. Look to your left. Do you see something that resembles the giant back of a chair?"

I cocked my head sideways until I spotted it. "Yes."

"That's your MMU."

"My what?"

"It's like a rocket backpack. It can take you wherever you want to go."

"How 'bout home?"

"If you follow my instructions, we'll all get there."

"But . . ." I swallowed. "I'm lousy at following instructions. That's how I wound up here in the first place. That's how you guys got locked inside that space station!"

"Well, you better start learning," Commander Phillips said. "Because it's the only way you can get us down. Now, cross over to the MMU."

I did.

"Pull down the control arms."

I did.

"Now back into it and take hold of the controls."

I didn't. "No way," I argued. "If I touch those controls I'll ruin them."

"No you won't. Not if you follow my instructions."

I sighed good and hard so he could hear me. I figured if you're going to die, it's good to let those responsible for your death know you're put out about it. I backed into the MMU, pulled down the arms, and took hold of the two controls, one for each hand. They were kind of like door handles that you could turn and swivel.

Commander Phillips continued. "The control in your right hand is your roll, pitch, and yaw command."

"My what?"

"If you twist it to the right you'll go upside down in a clockwise direction. To the left and—"

Before Commander Phillips could explain any more I gave the control a little turn. "This one here?" Suddenly I started spinning.

"*AUGH!*"

"WALLY!"

I grabbed the other control, the one for my left hand. I figured if the right sent me spinning, then the left would send me stopping. That's what I get for figuring. Instead of stopping, I shot out of the cargo bay spinning upside down, sideways, and every other way . . .

"*AUGH! AUGH!*"

"WALLY! WALLY!"

"*AUGH! AUGH! AUGH!*"

"WALLY! WALLY! WALLY!"

The conversation was getting a little boring, so I changed subjects and shouted, "WHAT DO I DO?"

"You've got to level off!"

"HOW?"

"Reverse the controls. Turn your right to the left and pull back on your left."

"MY RIGHT TO MY WHAT AND PULL MY LEFT TO WHO?"

"No! Your right hand, turn those controls to the left. And your left hand, pull that control back toward you."

I gave it a shot, and, after a few lifetimes passing before my eyes, I began to slow down.

"Okay," Commander Phillips said, "now ease up on the controls."

"No way!" I shouted. "I'm finally slowing down, why should I ruin it now by—"

"Wally, ease up! WALLY!"

For the slightest second everything stopped, but only for the slightest second. Suddenly, everything began to spin the other way as I started to shoot backwards.

"*AUGH! AUGH! AUGH!*"

"Wally, don't start that again."

"WHAT DO I DO?"

"Turn the controls back the other way. Only gently this time."

I twisted the controls back the other way, much more gently, and eased off when Commander Phillips said ease off. And, surprise of surprises, I was actually starting to float right side up again.

Ahead of me, I saw something white. At first I thought it was a meteor or satellite or something—until I noticed this particular meteor or satellite or something happened to have arms and legs.

"I see him," I shouted. "I see O'Brien!"

"Good."

Commander Phillips gave me more commands, and, after making a few hundred mistakes, I finally caught on. Eventually I was scooting toward O'Brien. But I was going just a little slower than I liked. So, without bothering to tell Commander Phillips, I pushed the controls forward so I could get there faster.

I made good headway. Pilot O'Brien was growing larger. Things were going great. O'Brien even gave me a friendly wave. At least I thought it was friendly. It wasn't until I was nearly on top of him that I realized he wasn't waving, "Hi there." He was waving, "Get back, get away, you're coming too fast!"

There were other clues, too, like his shouting: "Get back, get away, you're coming too fast!"

I threw the controls into reverse as quickly as I could, but it was too late. O'Brien's eyes widened in horror as he tried to swim out of the way. Nothing helped. I slammed into him like a freight train without brakes. His right shoulder kind of crumpled under the impact. He gave a little *OAF!* and suddenly went limp. I reached out and managed to grab him as we started to tumble and spin out of control.

"O'Brien!" I shouted. "O'Brien, can you hear me?"

He stirred and opened his eyes. I could tell he was hurting by the way he winced. He glanced to me and then looked down to the oxygen readout on his chest. Suddenly he seemed very concerned and motioned for me to look.

I did.

I wished I hadn't. For some reason, the guy had less than two hours of air left—and it was going fast! I watched as the readout dropped from:

1.8 . . . 1.7 . . . 1.6 . . .

"What's going on?" I asked.

He whispered hoarsely. "You must have ripped a tiny hole in my suit. I'm losing pressure. Get me back. Quick, get me back."

We were still tumbling out of control, farther and farther away from the *Encounter*.

I looked back down to his readout:

1.4 . . . 1.3 . . .

“What do I do?” I cried. “How do I turn us around!”

O’Brien could barely answer, the pain was so great. “Level us off. Turn us around and head back toward the shuttle.”

“But how do I—”

“You got out here, didn’t you?” he gasped. “Just take your time. Level off, *slowly*, and turn us around.”

With O’Brien practically sitting in my lap, things were a little tricky, but with his help I somehow managed to straighten us out. Then we turned around. But when we finally faced the shuttle, I almost lost it. The *Encounter* and Space Station One were farther away than I had imagined. I glanced to O’Brien, then to his readout:

1.1 . . . 1.0 . . .

I tried to fight back the panic, but it didn’t do much good. I knew we wouldn’t make it back in time.

Chapter 8

Recovery

I looked first to O'Brien's concerned face and then to his oxygen readout:

0.9 . . . 0.8 . . .

"We're not going to make it!" I said. "You're almost out of air."

"Push forward on the left control," he ordered. "Increase your speed, push us forward."

"Forget it," I answered. "That's how I got us in this jam in the first place. I was going too fast."

"Do it, Wilbur."

"I'll kill us."

"You'll kill me if you don't!" He caught himself and tried again, this time pretending to be more calm and relaxed. "You're going to have to push forward on the left control just as far as it will go."

I looked down to his readout:

0.6 . . . 0.5 . . .

I had no choice. I pushed forward on the handle, and we shot off.

"*WOOOOAHH* . . ."

"We're traveling at 66 feet per second," he said. "We'll be there in no time flat."

He was right. The *Encounter* came faster than I ever thought possible.

"Now ease back . . . pull her back. Not too hard. Easy does it now."

I threw another look to his pack:

0.4 . . . 0.3 . . .

"Slow us down just a little more."

We drifted over the shuttle bay doors.

"Now drop us in. Turn her around and drop us inside."

I banged and scraped a couple of things along the way (mostly Pilot O'Brien).

"Ow, Ooo, Ouch—Warren, are you doing this on purpose?"

I shook my head.

After a little doing (and a lot more banging) , we finally made it into the cargo bay.

0.2 . . .

It was going to be close. I slipped out of the jet pack and pulled O'Brien with me into the air lock. He helped as much as he could, which wasn't a lot.

"Okay," he said, "reach over to that AIRLOCK DEPRESS. Set it to: 10.2 PSI."

I did. We both looked down to his read out:

0.1 . . .

"Should I take off your helmet?" I asked.

"No, not yet."

"But—"

"Not yet! Wait until the green light above the control comes on."

I waited. Half the time watching for the green light, the other half watching his digital readout. It clicked to:

0.0

An alarm began to sound.

I moved for the helmet.

"No," he gasped, "wait for the green light!"

No way. I couldn't wait. O'Brien would suffocate. I had to get the helmet off. I started to reach for it, to unsnap it.

"No," he shook his head violently. "Follow my orders!"

Suddenly there was a loud hiss in the compartment and the green light glowed. I pulled off his helmet, and we both floated there several seconds catching our breath.

"Is everything okay in there?" Commander Phillips' voice asked.

"Yes," O'Brien gasped. "We made it." Then turning to me he scowled. "You're going to have to learn to start following orders."

I looked down a little embarrassed.

"Well, at least you waited for that green light before taking off my helmet."

I looked up. "Why, what would have happened?"

"You would have killed me."

I floated there in stunned silence. The words echoed in my head for a long time.

"Okay, Watson," O'Brien tried to move, but he was still in a lot of pain. "Let's get the crew compartment pressurized so we can get in."

I nodded and flipped the switches and knobs he called for. Soon we slid open the inside hatch that lead to the mid deck.

Ah . . . home, sweet space shuttle.

We got out of our suits. At last I could straighten my glasses. O'Brien seemed to do more than his fair share of wincing and grimacing. I was also doing plenty of it—but not over physical pain. It was more like, mental stupidity. Would I ever catch on? Would I ever learn to just follow the rules?

Commander Phillips suggested we rest a few hours before tackling the next job. I had no idea what that would be and didn't particularly want to ask. After all we'd been through, taking a little rest was one order I definitely planned to obey.

Unfortunately I couldn't get my mind to shut down. So, doing what I always do to help me relax, I reached for ol' Betsy and continued my latest superhero story.

When we last left Neutron Dude, he was about to be turned into a giant turnip (or something equally as tasteless) by the notoriously, not-so-nice...Veggie-Man.

"Be reasonable," our hero cries as he backs away. "Think of the kids. How can you ask them to eat nothing but fruits and vegetables for the rest of their lives? It's too unfair. It's too unjust. Their taste buds will go through withdrawal."

"Too bad," the sinister scum snarls. "Soon the entire world will be nothing but one giant health-food store."

He lifts up his creepy can of Health

Spray and is about to fire.... Suddenly, Neutron Dude has an idea. Before you can say, "I knew he'd come up with something, these superhero types always do," Dude reaches into his back pocket and pulls out a giant bag of deep-fried, extra-crunchy, Chipper Chippy Chips. The one he keeps handy for just such emergencies.

Veggie-Man lets out a gasp. "Where did you get those?" he cries. "I thought I destroyed all junk food!"

Without a word, Neutron Dude tears into the bag and pops one of the heavenly-tasting, artery pluggers into his mouth.

"AUGH!" Veggie-Man screams. "Stop it, you're killing yourself."

Neutron Dude grins as he crams another handful into his mouth. And then another. And another.

Veggie-Man is beside himself. He begins to tremble, then to quiver, then to shake, rattle, and roll. It's been years since he's seen such awful eating habits. But, mustering all of his bad-guy badness, he manages to raise the Health Spray and fire a single burst at the bag of chips.

Nothing happens.

Neutron Dude grins and continues cramming handful after handful of the grease-covered, heart-stopping delicacies into his mouth.

Veggie-Man screams. "STOP IT! STOP IT!" With trembling hands he fires still another blast of the Health Spray.

Still nothing.

"What have you done?" he screams. "What's wrong with my Health Spray? It's supposed to turn everything into fruits and vegetables!"

Neutron Dude answers,*"MMURRFF MOOMMERF FRUMMMMERRR."*

"What?"

With his mouth crammed full, Neutron Dude simply points to the words on his bag: *Potato Chips.*

Great green beans! Holy huckleberries! (And you thought I'd run out of these.) Veggie-Man suddenly realizes that somewhere amidst all of the grease and salt in that bag there are actual microscopic pieces of potatoes. And, as we all know, potatoes are...drum roll, please... vegetables!

"NO!" Veggie-Man screams. "IT'S NOT POSSIBLE, I'VE BEEN HOODWINKED!"

Our hero tosses away the empty potato chip bag and reaches into another pocket.

"Now what? Veggie-Man cries.

Neutron Dude McDoogle pulls out a different type of bag and tears it open.

Veggie-Man fires off more Health Spray.

More of nothing happens.

Neutron Dude smiles and turns the bag around to reveal the words: *Corn Chips.*

"OF COURSE!" Veggie-Man gasps. Corn is a vegetable, too.

Neutron Dude continues grinning and chomping away on the goodies.

"Please!" Veggie-Man drops to his knees. "Please, I beg you...don't eat any more of that awful junk in front of me...."

Filled with compassion and understanding (something they teach the good guys in the best good-guy schools), Neutron Dude lowers his bag.

But, it's a trick! (Something they teach the baddest bad guys in the baddest bad-guy schools). Veggie-Man points his spray at the tiled floor and fires. Suddenly the tiles melt into pools of safflower oil. Neutron Dude's feet slip out from under him and he falls to the floor, dropping the chips.

Now Veggie-Man goes in for the kill. With all his chips out of reach, Neutron Dude has no defense. In a matter of seconds the world will be reduced to nothing but fruits and vegetables. Soon, kids will be blowing out candles on birthday cantalopes. They'll be going to the fair and eating cotton-candied cauliflower, watching movies while munching on hot, freshly buttered radishes.

Closer and closer Veggie-Man comes. He aims his spray directly at our hero's skull and sneers. "So, how would you like to become the first living Mr. Potato Head?"

And then, when all appears lost—

"Wally? O'Brien?" It was Commander Phillips' voice. He was still over at the space station. With their hatch broken and sealed shut, there weren't a lot of places he could be.

"I've just talked with Control. They feel the best thing to do is scrub this mission and send up the next shuttle with appropriate tools and crew to pry open our hatch and rescue us."

"You guys have enough provisions to last that long?" O'Brien asked.

"Plenty. The *Atlantis* is planned for a launch soon. They'll get us out, and we'll hitch a ride home with them. Unfortunately, it means you'll have to bring the *Encounter* down on your own."

"We might have a problem with that, Skipper," O'Brien said.

"How so?"

"My arm is pretty banged up. I don't have much use of my right hand."

"You have Wally there. He can help."

Pilot O'Brien and I exchanged looks. Finally he pressed his intercom button and said what we were both thinking.

"I don't know if *help* is the right word, Commander."

"Well, it'll have to be. McDoogle will have to help you land the shuttle. It's our only option."

I swallowed hard. Well, at least I wanted to swallow hard. Unfortunately, at the moment, my swallower didn't have much to swallow.

Chapter 9

Homeward Bound . . . Maybe

"Okay, Willy," O'Brien sighed. "Leaving orbit and reentering the atmosphere is the most critical phase of the flight. You have to listen to my orders. One foul-up and we become human charcoal."

I nodded, trying my best to pay attention, but at the same time wondering when I'd have time to write out my Last Will and Testament.

"First, we have to store all the equipment. When I fire up the engines to slow us down, things will shift radically."

I nodded and started to work. I stored everything exactly as he said. Well, everything except ol' Betsy. I had to keep her handy. I knew I wasn't exactly following every order, but what harm could a little 5.3-pound laptop computer do?

I'd soon find out.

We climbed into some pants with a bunch of air

bags stitched into the legs. "They're Anti-G suits," he explained. "We're traveling at 17,300 miles an hour. When we slow down, all the blood in our bodies will rush down from our head to our feet. By inflating the air bags in these trousers, we'll keep the blood in our upper body so we won't pass out."

I quickly slipped on the pants. The last thing in the world a guy wants to do in the middle of dying is to pass out. I mean, what if you get to heaven and they have all these accident forms you have to fill out?

After closing the cargo bay doors, we strapped into our seats—O'Brien in the commander's chair, and me to his right in the pilot's chair. It felt kinda cool, like being in one of those sit-down jet-fighter video games. Although this time I didn't expect to be firing any rockets or doing any fancy flying.

Wrong again.

O'Brien grabbed a couple of notebooks and handed one to me. "These cue cards give us the step-by-step on what to do. Most of it's handled by computer, but we still have to fly a little ourselves."

He loaded the "Landing Program" into the computer and grabbed the control stick in front of him. It was just like the one I had in front of me. Slowly, he maneuvered the stick and turned the *Encounter* completely around. Soon we were at the exact angle the numbers on the computer screen called for.

"I've turned her around so when we burn the engines, we'll slow down. Of course we'll have to turn her back after the burn." He switched a couple hundred more switches and pressed the intercom button: "Control, this is *Encounter*. OMS engines are armed."

"Roger," came the answer, "OMS armed."

"Well, here goes," he said. "Once I press this button and those engines fire, there's no turning back."

I nodded.

He reached for the computer keyboard and pressed the EXEC key. I reached for the arms of my chair and held on tight.

More numbers appeared on the computer screen, and O'Brien pressed his intercom button to read them out loud. "Control, this is *Encounter*. Countdown to OMS burn in five, four, three, two, one . . ."

There was that old, familiar *WHOMP* sound of the engines firing, the same *WHOMP* that sent me crashing into the wall with my juice just a day earlier. Fortunately, this time I was strapped into my seat, safe and sound. Unfortunately, ol' Betsy was not. As we suddenly slowed, Betsy suddenly floated into view and started flying toward the back wall.

I had to catch her. We'd been through too many adventures together to let her be smashed into tiny micro bits. I lunged for her, and managed to bat her back in our direction. Well, actually, in O'Brien's direction.

"Willy!" he shouted as he turned toward me, "What are you—"

AUGH!
K-LUNK
UH-OH

The *AUGH*! was what he said as he saw ol' Betsy speeding toward his forehead.

The *K-LUNK* was the sound ol' Betsy made when she hit his forehead.

The *UH-OH* was my realizing maybe I should have followed his orders just a little closer and stored ol' Betsy away. I grabbed my computer and shouted, "Mr. O'Brien, Mr. O'Brien, are you all right?"

If the guy was all right, he wasn't letting anyone in on the secret. His eyes were closed and his arms floated up like he was unconscious or something. My incredible intellect put together all these facts and came up to the staggering conclusion:

HE *WAS* UNCONSCIOUS OR SOMETHING!

"Mr. O'Brien," I cried, "Mr. O'Brien, wake up!"

No answer.

"Mr. O'Brien!"

"Wally," it was Commander Phillips' voice. "Wally, are you all right?"

"It's O'Brien, he's unconscious!"

There was no answer. I quickly secured ol' Betsy and shouted, "Commander Phillips, what do I do? How do I shut this thing off!"

Another long pause and then a very short answer. "You don't."

"What?"

"Once you commence OMS you must continue your descent."

"But I don't know how to land this thing!"

"You're going to have to learn."

"But—"

"I'll talk you through it. I'll be right here with you the whole time."

"That's what we tried with the jet pack!" I cried, "You saw how I fouled that up!"

"That's because you weren't following my instructions. Wally, you must listen to everything I say. You must follow every word to the letter. Don't do *anything* different than what I say, don't *think* anything different, don't *breathe* anything different. Do I make myself clear?"

"Yeah, but—"

"I know you've had trouble following instructions before, but if you don't obey this time . . ." he paused.

"What?" I cried, "what will happen if I don't obey?"

He answered quietly. "Then you'll never have a chance to obey again."

I caught his drift. No more fooling around. I was determined to follow every single direction, obey every single command. I was also determined to ask for a little help . . .

Dear God, I silently prayed, *I've sure been messing things up. No matter how hard I try, I keep breaking some rule or another. Please . . . help me. Help me do right. Help me follow the instructions.*

"What are you doing?" Commander Phillips asked.

"I, uh . . . I was praying."

There was a pause and another quiet answer. "That sounds like a good idea, Wally. That sounds like a good idea for all of us . . ."

After a moment he came back on. "Okay, Wally. Listen very carefully. We'll get you down, but you'll have to trust me. Do you see that flight stick in front of you—the one identical to O'Brien's?"

"You mean the one that looks like it's from a video arcade?"

"That's the one. Do you play a lot of video arcade games?"

"Sure, all the time."

"That's good news."

"In fact I have the reputation for spending more quarters than anybody just to get the worst score."

His silence said that maybe it wasn't such good news.

I cleared my throat. "I take it we don't have any spare quarters?"

"That's right, Wally. No spare quarters. We've got one time and one time only to do this right."

I took a deep breath and waited for my instructions.

After a long talk with Control, Commander Phillips had me switch a bunch of switches. He told me exactly where they were and exactly when they should be switched. I obeyed every word.

No more foul-ups.

Not this time.

Next he had me enter some numbers and stuff into the shuttle's computer. Again, no problem.

"Okay, Wally, this next step is a little tricky. We're going to have to turn the shuttle around nose first. So, take hold of the stick in front of you and gently, *very gently,* push it toward the lower left."

I took the stick and did exactly as he said.

"Slowly . . . slowly . . ."

Sure enough, the shuttle started to turn.

"Slowly . . ." he kept saying, "nice and slowly . . ." Now, I don't know what got into me, but after a few eternities of this "slowly" stuff I could clearly see what Commander Phillips was doing. I could clearly see where I was heading and where we were going. So I figured I could help him along a little. Not a lot. Just a little. By pushing the stick just a little farther to the left, we'd be done just a little sooner.

I know, I know . . . I wasn't exactly following the program, and I should probably have my head checked for a brain, especially after all I'd been through. But this was so easy. All I did was move the stick another half inch. It wasn't a big deal. He wouldn't even know. I just wanted to give him a helpful hand.

"Wally! You're turning too fast! Pull it to the right!"

So much for helpful hands. I pulled the stick to the right. Unfortunately, it was just a little too hard, just a little too fast. It was just like being in the jet pack all over again! Only this time it was the entire shuttle that began to twist and turn in the wrong direction.

"What's going on?" I shouted. "What did I do?"

I could see the Earth's horizon coming up in the

window. It was followed by more space, which was followed by more Earth again.

"You've put her into spin!" Commander Phillips called. "Wally, you've put her into a spin! You've got to pull out of it!"

I yanked the control stick the other direction, which only made things worse.

"No . . . Wally . . . you're overcompensating."

"But I've got to stop it!"

"Put the stick back into its neutral position."

"But I've got to—"

"Now, Wally! Put the stick back!"

"But—"

"NOW!"

It was against my better judgment, but I finally did what Phillips said.

And, just as I suspected, nothing happened. I looked out the window and saw the Earth and outer space still doing their tumbling routine.

I had to do something. I had to stop it. I reached for the stick. But, as if reading my mind, Commander Phillips shouted. "No, Wally, do what I say . . . obey me!"

With all of my willpower (and maybe some extra from above) I was able to pull my hands away.

Commander Phillips came back on. "Now, gently place your hands on the stick. *Gently.*"

I did.

We were still spinning.

"Push up and to the right . . . gently."

I did, but nothing happened. The spinning grew worse. I wanted desperately to push more. "Commander Phill—"

"Trust me! It will level off! Just hold it there."

I fought against everything I felt. I fought against the tumbling, the raw panic, and the knowledge that I had a free video rental coupon at home that I'd never be able to redeem.

It was an incredible struggle, but, somehow, some way I was able to keep listening and obeying. I was able to do everything he ordered.

"Gently . . . hold it . . . hold it . . ."

And gradually, ever so gradually . . . the tumbling began to slow.

"Nice and easy, now . . . hold it . . . we're almost there."

I resisted the temptation to put on some finishing touches. As far as I could tell we didn't need any more of my touches.

"And now . . . ease up. Nice and slow."

I did.

Peeking out the window, I was relieved to see the Earth and horizon had finally stopped their acrobatics. I took a deep breath and slowly let it out.

I heard Commander Phillips do the same.

"Sorry," I said. "It won't happen again."

"It better not, because we have one more maneuver coming up."

"One more!"

"That's right, and you won't have me around to make sure you do it correctly."

"What are you talking about?

"You're about to reenter the atmosphere. The outside of *Encounter* will heat up to 1500 degrees Celsius. You won't be able to communicate with anyone for twelve minutes."

"Twelve minutes!"

"Relax. Just do everything I say and follow the readouts on your computer screen. If you do, everything will be fine."

I took another deep breath and wiped my hands. This following the rules business seemed to be getting more and more intense. Granted, I was learning, but I still wasn't batting a thousand. And by the looks of things, a thousand is exactly what I needed to do to get home alive.

"Look down at the computer screen, Wally. Do you see a little outline of the shuttle?"

"I see two. One's pointed up, the other's kind of straight."

"The straight one is you. You need to pull up on your nose until your shuttle fits perfectly over the outline of the other."

"Why would I want to point up if we're heading down?"

"It will slow you and allow your heat tiles to absorb the heat. You must point that nose up between 28 and 38 degrees."

I still didn't understand but figured it wouldn't hurt to keep doing things his way. "Okay," I said. "When should I start?"

"Now."

"What?"

"Not too fast, but gradually pull your stick up into that 28 to 38 degree position."

"But—"

"Wally . . ." His voice was already starting to fade and crackle. "Pull that nose up, exactly like that diagram, or you'll burn up."

"What if I can't?" I waited for an answer, but there was none. "Commander Phillips?" I heard some words but couldn't make them out. "Commander Phillips? Commander Phillips!"

Now there was nothing but static.

And then I saw it. The glow. Outside, around the hull. It was kind of red and orangish. We were already starting to reenter the Earth's atmosphere. Things were already starting to heat up.

I looked back to the computer screen. The number beside our shuttle read 12. Commander Phillips had said I had to be between 28 and 38.

I quickly pulled back on the stick.

Gently, his voice echoed in my mind.

I eased up and pulled more slowly.

14 . . . 16 . . . 17 . . .

It was harder than I thought.

The shuttle started to vibrate. “What’s wrong?” I shouted. “Commander Phillips?”

No answer. Nothing but static. I threw a look to O’Brien. He was still out.

The vibrating grew worse until it turned into violent shakings. I had to be doing something wrong. I had to be! I let up on the stick. We dropped back:

17 . . . 16 . . .

The shaking grew even worse. The red glow outside became brighter and brighter.

“We’re burning up!” I cried. “I have to let up more!”

NO! my thoughts cried back. *HE SAID 28 TO 38 DEGREES.*

I looked to the computer screen. I was way off. That’s it! That’s why I was burning up! I had to obey. Even if it didn’t make sense, I had to pull the nose up to at least 28 degrees.

I tugged harder on the stick.

17 . . . 23 . . . 26 . . .

We were almost there, but the vibrating and shaking didn't stop. In fact they grew worse. So did the noise. It was a rushing roar. I stopped pulling, afraid I was doing something wrong, afraid I was killing us.

NO! HE SAID 28 TO 38 DEGREES! HE SAID FOLLOW THE COMPUTER!

I looked to the screen. We were down to 24. I started pulling again:

25 . . . 27 . . . 28 . . .

Our shuttle diagram was almost identical to the one on the computer screen.

I began to let up.

26 . . . 25 . . .

NO! AT LEAST 28 DEGREES.

I pulled the stick. It was hard with all the shaking and bouncing, but he had said 28 to 38 degrees, and if that's what he wanted, that's what he would get.

28 . . . 30 . . . 31 . . . 34 . . .

I don't know how long I fought the stick. It was like a nightmare that wouldn't stop. It seemed the more I tried to follow Commander Phillips' orders, the worse things got. But I'd seen enough of what happened when I did things my way. This time it would be his way or nothing. I'd follow his orders, I'd obey the computer readout. Even if it killed us, I would obey.

And then, suddenly, the roar and shaking began to stop.

I looked out the window. The fiery glow was going, too. Instead of the blackness of outer space, we were surrounded by blue—a blue that was getting lighter by the second.

O'Brien groaned. I looked over to him. He shook his head and mumbled, "Where are we?"

Before I could answer, the radio crackled to life. "*Encounter*, this is Control. *Encounter* this is Control, do you copy?"

O'Brien blinked his eyes a couple of times to get his bearings. Then he sat up and checked some of the readouts.

"*Encounter*, this is Control, do you copy?"

Finally he reached for the intercom switch. "Roger Control, this is *Encounter*. We are commencing

S turn maneuvers and moving speed brake back to 100%."

"We copy, *Encounter*. You're looking good."

Soon, O'Brien was back in the swing of things, flipping switches, and taking control of the stick. He had only a second to look over to me. I couldn't tell if he was amazed or just plain shocked. Maybe it was both. He said only one sentence, but it was one of the best sentences I'd ever heard.

"Don't just sit there, *Wally*, give me a hand."

I looked to him and grinned.

I'm not sure, but I think he actually grinned back.

Chapter 10

Wrapping Up

The rest of the landing went pretty smooth. I just flipped the switches O'Brien said to flip and pushed the buttons O'Brien said to push. It was a piece of cake. I guess when you get down to it, obeying rules does make things a little easier.

It was pretty cool looking out the window and seeing Florida come into view. It was even cooler when we saw the runway. O'Brien made one last turn, straightened us out, then set us up for the landing. Now we were just like any old jetliner coming into any old airport . . . except for the sound. There was none. Just rushing wind.

"Why's that?" I asked.

"Because we don't have any power," he said.

"What?"

"Relax, that's how we're designed. We've been gliding ever since we left orbit."

I shook my head in surprise and amazement.

When we were just a few feet above the landing strip, O'Brien raised the cover of the landing gear switch and snapped it on.

Then a voice from Control came over the radio: "*Encounter*, main gear at ten feet, five feet, three feet, two feet, one . . . contact."

The shuttle gave a slight jolt as our back wheels hit the ground.

"Nose wheel at five feet, four, three, two, one . . . contact."

Another jolt as our front wheels came down.

And finally the words . . . "Welcome home, *Encounter*."

"Roger," O'Brien said, "It's good to be back."

He flipped a switch that popped out a parachute to slow us down. Thirty seconds later we rolled to a stop. I threw a look over to him. After all we'd been through, I could feel a sense of friendship between us. It was one of those deep, unspoken, male bonding things.

"That wasn't so bad," I grinned. "Maybe we could do it again sometime."

O'Brien just looked at me, then went back to flipping switches as he muttered, "Not in this lifetime, Waldo."

So much for male bonding.

I grabbed ol' Betsy and rose from my chair. As I

crossed to the ladder and climbed down to the mid deck, my body felt like it weighed a ton.

"It's the gravity," O'Brien explained as he cracked open the hatch, squinted at the sunlight, and started down the stairs toward the waiting crowd. "It'll take a little while to get your coordination back."

I wanted to explain that it's taken me thirteen years, and I still didn't quite have it down. But my first step onto the stairway saved me the trouble. Something about the way I tumbled head over heels and crashed onto the pavement face-first seemed to make my point. Then, of course, there were all those TV cameras that showed my grace to the entire world . . . just in case anybody still had their doubts.

Wall Street and Opera were the first at my side. "Oh Wally, Wally!" they shouted.

"So how's that movie deal?" I asked Wall Street. "Did I make enough blunders?"

"Forget the movie deal," she said. "Some toy guys are inventing a new doll. It's called, *Little Wally Crash 'N Burn.*"

"What does it do?" I asked.

"You just hold it in your hand and for no reason at all it falls over and explodes. We'll make millions!"

Next came Mom doing her usual hugging and crying-because-she's-so-happy routine.

Finally, there was Dad. Part of me wanted to hug him, but part of me knew he wouldn't want to show that kind of emotion in front all those lights and cameras. Luckily he saved me the bother by suddenly sticking out his manly hand for a manly handshake. "Welcome back, son." I knew a handshake was the best he could come up with under the circumstances, so I grabbed his hand and squeezed it for all I was worth. "Oh, Dad," I said, starting to tear up. "I'm so glad to be home!"

"I'm uh, I'm glad your home, too, son." He put his hand on my shoulder and gave a slight squeeze.

I could tell by the thickness in his voice that he was really touched and that he really wanted to express his feelings. I could also tell by the way he was glancing at all the cameras and people that it would be really tough on him.

"It's okay, Dad," I said. "You can tell me what you're really thinking."

Finally, he spoke. "Well, son . . . the parking here is $2.75 an hour. We've already been here one hour. But if we hurry they might not charge us for the second."

I laughed. Good ol' Dad. Some things never change. He shrugged and gave a half smile.

We all turned and started for the parking lot. Of course there would be lots of things to straighten out with NASA—mostly about how many zillions of lawns I'd have to mow to pay them back for my little "Learn-to-Follow-the Rules" field trip.

Later, at the motel room, we watched Commander Phillips on the news. He was up in Space Station One talking about how he wasn't worried and how the next shuttle would be taking off in a couple of weeks to rescue them. When my name came up, he just grinned and said, "Yes sir, that Wally McDoogle is quite a trooper. I'm looking forward to the day when he can become a real, official astronaut." What he didn't mention was that he hoped to be retired and on the other side of the planet if that day should ever arrive.

It was getting late and everybody decided to hit the hay. Everybody but me. I was still wound up, so I pulled out ol' Betsy to try to finish up my little Neutron Dude story. . . .

Veggie-Man, the horrendously healthy health nut, hovers over our heroically helpless hero (say that seven times fast). He is about to turn Neutron Dude into somebody's version of a veggie platter. But just before he fires the can of Health Spray, the roof to his laboratory explodes. Bits and pieces of

ceiling fall all around them as a space shuttle breaks through the rafters and glides into a perfect landing atop one of the giant lab counters.

The hatch opens and out pops Commander Phillips, followed by Payload Specialist Meyer and Missions Specialist Dr. Lambert.

"Wait a minute!" Veggie-Man cries. "Your story is over! You can't come barging into this one!"

"Why not?" Commander Phillips asks as he leaps to the ground and straightens his flight suit.

"It's not fair," Veggie-Man shouts. "Our author can't go around mixing reality with his superhero stories."

"Says who?" asks Dr. Lambert.

"It's against the rules," Veggie-Man complains.

"Precisely," Commander Phillips agrees. "But since you're not following the bad-guy rules, why should our writer, the great and always-brilliant Wally McDoogle, follow the writing rules?"

"What are you talking about?" Veggie-Man whines. "I'm following the bad-guy rules to the letter. Check it out for yourself." He pulls a book off the shelf and tosses it to Dr. Lambert. It's the latest edition of the Bad-Guys Rule Book. She quickly flips to the chapter entitled, "Super Villain."

"Aren't I being sinisterly slimy?" he asks.

"Check," she says.

"And villainously vile?"

"Double check."

"And my breath?" He burps and blows some of the organic fumes in her direction. "Doesn't it meet all the bad-guy bad-breath requirements?"

She coughs and gags. "Check again."

"So what rule am I breaking?"

Commander Phillips explains. "Bad guys are supposed to do bad things."

"I'm turning everything into health food. Isn't that bad enough?"

Phillips shakes his head. "No, that's good."

"What are you talking about?"

Neutron Dude steps in. "I think I see their point Veggie-Man. By creating food that's healthy to eat, you're actually doing something good."

"Which means," Dr. Lambert says, tapping her manual, "you're breaking a major bad-guy rule."

"Oh no!" Veggie-Man gasps.

"Oh yes," Phillips says. "By being bad, you're actually being good."

Veggie-Man breaks into a cold sweat. "What do I do? How can I change my ways?"

Everyone is stumped until Neutron Dude (still being the hero of our story which, of course, means he has to have the answer), suddenly has...you guessed it...the answer. "Since we're all in the same McDoogle book, maybe you can ask Wally to introduce you to one of the bad-guys from his real-life story."

"That's right," Dr. Lambert agrees, "Like that chubby boy who's always eating."

"You mean, Opera?"

"Yeah, he has a bad junk food habit."

Phillips nods. "Or that other friend of his who's always trying to make a buck off him?"

Meyer shakes his head. "No, they're both too good. Hey, I've got it! How 'bout Mad Dog Miller? You know, that

hockey player from Wally's *My Life as a Human Hockey Puck* book? He was pretty bad."

"Or those pirates from *My Life as a Torpedo Test Target?*" Phillips says.

"Or those Save the Snail terrorists from *My Life as Dinosaur Dental Floss?*"

"Or, how 'bout—"

And so the group goes on. Each trying to give Veggie-Man examples of how following bad-guy rules can make him the best at being the baddest. For as we all know, rules are important to follow, no matter who you are.

"Or, how 'bout those poachers Wally ran into in *My Life as Crocodile Junk Food*? Or those balloon racers from *My Life as a Broken Bungee Cord?* Or that mechanical monster in..."

I stopped typing and looked up from the screen. My eyes were getting weak, and my mind was getting tired (or maybe it was the other way around). In any case, I pressed F10 to save the story and shut ol' Betsy down for the night. I figured, like me, Veggie-Man had definitely learned his lesson about following rules. (Besides I was getting tired of working in all that free advertising for my other books.)

I gave a hearty stretch and closed my eyes. With any luck, I was done with these crazy adventures for a while. With any luck I had gone through enough disasters and catastrophes.

Then again, we all know about my luck. . . .